Reckoning Tide

Reckoning Tide

Anneli Purchase

ACQUILINE

Copyright © 2015 by Anneli Purchase

All rights reserved, including the right of reproduction whole or in part in any form

Manufactured in the United States of America

Published in 2015 by Acquiline

Library and Archives Canada Cataloguing in Publication

Purchase, Anneli, 1947-, author
        Reckoning tide / Anneli Purchase.

Issued in print and electronic formats.
ISBN 978-0-9947557-3-5 (bound).

        I. Title.

PS8631.U73R43 2015   C813'.6   C2015-904270-4

This book is dedicated to my two most valued writer-friends Darlene Jones and Kathleen Price. You're the best!

Acknowledgements

This sequel to The Wind Weeps has taken shape over a long period of time. It is only because of the support and gentle nudging of my friends and family that it has finally reached completion. I've learned that a follow up novel is more of a challenge than the original, as readers are bound to compare, but although this sequel continues from the point where The Wind Weeps stops, it is nevertheless its own story.

Many of the scenes take place on or around fishboats and in marine environments. I was fortunate to have at hand the nautical expertise of my husband to make sure I used the correct terms for anything related to boats and the coast.

My writing buddy, Darlene Jones, has given me many hours of her valuable time and expertise in the substantive editing aspect of the novel. I would still be struggling with many writing issues if not for her intuitive guidance and insights.

I owe huge thanks to my friend, Kathleen Price, who is always there for me. Her experience and skills in copy-editing, book design and layout, and writerly advice have helped to make the publishing process much easier for me.

~

You're mine!
To have,
To hold,
No matter how hard.

You're mine!
Give me honour,
Obey,
And do as you're told.

You're mine!
In sickness,
My sickness,
Comes hell.

You're mine!
This day forward,
'Til death,
Do us part.

~

Chapter 1

Nurse!" I screamed. "Nurse, come back!" Robert's smile vanished. He advanced and tossed the three orchids onto the foot of my bed.

I twisted around grasping for the cord with the call button. "Get away from me!" I hit the button frantically.

Robert lunged at me. "No, Andrea. Don't!" He ripped the cord away from me. I pulled my fist back to punch him, but he was quick and caught my wrist in an iron grip. His eyes narrowed into slits.

"Nurse!" I yelled again. He clamped a hand over my mouth. Flashbacks of what that hard hand had done to me went through my mind. I bit down on his fingers, my terror lending me extra strength.

"Arrrgh! You bitch!" Robert's eyes grew wide. He stared at me with a glassy look that I remembered too well. He drew his arm across his chest to backhand me, but dropped it when the nurse appeared.

"What's going on here?" the nurse demanded. Margaret was a hefty woman. She filled most of the doorway as she stood with her hands on her hips. "Sir! Come away from the bed."

"She bit me!" he said, unable to keep the whine out of his voice. "I brought her flowers—orchids, her favourite kind—and she bit me!"

I gasped at his outrageous boldfaced ploy, twisting the truth. "He tried to kill me. Don't let him near me. He's the one I told you about."

"Now, Andrea." Robert's voice, silky smooth, sent ripples of terror up my spine. "You know that's not true." He turned to the nurse and slowly shook his head. "I'm her husband. You see, she's had quite a shock. We had an argument and she set fire to our cabin and ran away when she thought I had died in the fire. I guess she's surprised to see that I'm still alive."

The nerve of him! I tried to get out of bed. "No! No-no-no!" I had to get the nurse to believe me. "He's twisting it all around. *He* tried to kill *me*."

The nurse was quick to put her hand out. "Stay in bed, Andrea." She looked flustered and tried to calm us both. But no wonder she was confused. The whole situation was so bizarre. She looked from Robert to me and back to Robert again.

Would she side with Robert?

"Sir," she said, "would you mind going to the waiting room down the hall? I'm sure the RCMP would like to speak with you, too. They'll be here soon to interview Andrea."

Robert raised his chin and gave me a smirk. "That was fast," he said. "We'll soon get to the bottom of the situation then."

The nurse escorted him out the door. "We called them this morning when she woke up," I heard her say as they walked down the hall.

The nurse had explained to me earlier that the police have to make a report in cases where there has been violence, especially since a gun was found in my fanny pack. *The gun I pointed at him last week. Should have pulled the damn trigger.*

The cup of herbal tea Margaret had brought me sat half empty when I woke up to her voice. "Andrea, wake up. The RCMP constable is here to talk to you."

"Huh? What time is it? How long have I been asleep?"

"Just a couple of hours," Margaret said. "Nothing wrong with getting some rest. You've had a tough time of it. Here's a hot facecloth. That'll feel good on your face and freshen you up. Then I'll bring the constable in."

The policewoman might have been a few years older than me, maybe thirty. She had a kind face, no makeup, and blondish hair pulled back and done up in some kind of knot. "I'm Constable Andersen. How are you feeling, Andrea?" She flipped open her notebook and clicked her pen.

"Much better knowing you're here." I tried to look past her towards the door. "Is Robert still out there?"

"No. The nurse said she'd asked him to wait, but there was no one in the waiting room. She's gone to have a quick look around. She was surprised. Said he seemed eager to tell his side of the story."

"Ha! I'm not surprised. He was just trying to brazen it out so people would think he's the victim here. But he ran because he knows the truth will come out and he's feeling very guilty."

"About?" Constable Andersen sat in the chair beside the bed.

"He tried to kill me. He locked me in our cabin, splashed gasoline on the walls and set fire to it." Tears leaked out as I relived that terrifying moment. It annoyed me that my hands were trembling. I reminded myself that I was going to be stronger from now on. I gave my head a little shake. "But I was able to climb out the bedroom window and make a run for it."

The policewoman's eyes opened wider and she stopped writing in her notebook. I was afraid she wouldn't believe me. "Is that what you were doing when the kayaker found you on the beach? Running away?"

"Yes. I knew he'd kill me if I stayed with him any longer."

"Why would he do that?" The constable was scribbling busily in her notebook again.

"Because he's crazy. He flies off the handle over the slightest thing. He's not stable, you know."

"In what way?"

"Well, he seems really charming at first, but anything at all can set him off." I shuddered. "Like the time he smashed me in the face when I giggled because the mousetrap had caught his thumb."

"Had he ever hit you before that?"

"All the time."

"All the time?"

"Well, not at first. You see we weren't married very long, barely a year. At first, he seemed really nice, but it turns out that when he gets mad, he hits."

The policewoman frowned. "Couldn't you tell anyone?"

"Who? The cabin was isolated. Like remote. Up the coast, way north of Powell River. My neighbours were cougars and bears. He could hit me as much as he wanted out there. And he did."

The constable's lips were pressed together. Her eyes squinted slightly and she breathed out through her nose.

"He did see a psychiatrist in Powell River sometimes, and he seemed to be better for a while afterwards." A shudder shook my body. "But it never lasted very long and he'd go crazy again, hitting me and yelling at me."

She scribbled in her notebook some more. "I see. Now there's one thing that bothers me. The kayaker who found you unconscious on the beach said you had a handgun in your fanny pack. Can you explain that?"

I let out a long sigh. "That was Robert's gun. He said to keep it in the fanny pack when I was out mushroom picking or going for a walk out there because of the animals. I never used it, but I felt safer having it just in case."

"How did you come to have it with you on the beach?"

"I grabbed my fanny pack before I climbed out the window. It has all my survival gear in it. Including the gun."

"I understand it's different when you live alone in the bush. Still, we'll have to confiscate the gun because you had it illegally. I don't think there's any need for charges because of the extenuating circumstances."

I wasn't planning on going back into the bush anyway, so I was glad enough to give up the gun as long as I didn't get charged with any weapons offence. "Okay. Thanks. I wouldn't have hurt anyone with it, but I won't let Robert hurt me again. I'll never let anyone hurt me again." I looked down at my hands. They were balled up into fists. I had to force myself to relax them to look normal. "Isn't there anything you can do about Robert? Arrest him or something?"

"For?"

Hadn't she heard anything I said? "For trying to kill me? For beating me half to death? For being a maniac?"

"The injuries and bruises you have now could be from your recent days in the woods. The fire in the cabin— it'll be your word against his. And as for the instability, there's no law against being mean or unpredictable."

My jaw dropped. "So there's nothing you can do?"

"You can apply for a restraining order." She shrugged. "That way he won't be allowed to be within a certain distance of your residence. He won't be allowed to contact you, or bother you in any way, but they don't always work." She put her hand on mine. "Your best bet is to keep out of his way."

"So in other words, there's nothing you can do—not really."

"Not really."

"I can't believe this. I've been beaten up for a year and there's nothing you can do about it."

We looked at each other in silence. Finally I sighed and said, "If I get a restraining order what happens if he doesn't stick to the order?"

"Then you call us right away and we'll deal with him."

That'll be way too late. "Okay. Thanks." My fists were forming again, but my stomach was churning. I knew there was no way Robert would listen to any kind of orders from anyone. It was just a matter of time before he came after me again.

Constable Andersen closed her notebook. "What will you do now?" she asked.

My head jerked up and I took a quick breath. "Ah ... er...." My brow wrinkled as I tried to think. "I'm not sure. My friend Jim is coming to see me. I'll decide then." I hoped he would still want me. If not, I was basically alone and homeless without a penny to my name.

Chapter 2

The next day I woke up feeling groggy, struggling to make my brain work, struggling to remember where I was and why I was in bed with sunlight streaming in through the window. Why wasn't I up and ... doing what? Where was I anyway? Slowly, memories formed in my scrambled mind—hospital. Why was I here anyway? I was running away.... Robert—Robert! I lifted my head off the pillow with a cry.

I glanced around the room trying to orient myself. Oh my God! There he was! Behind the curtain! I could see his legs sprawling out from a chair in the corner near the foot of my bed. He must have heard me. He was getting up. I opened my mouth to call for the nurse again when I heard him say, "Sh-sh-sh, Andrea. It's okay. You're safe."

"Huh?" I knew that voice, that face. "Jim?" Was I awake yet? Maybe I was dreaming. I scrunched my eyes shut and opened them again. "Is it really you, Jim?"

He rubbed my arm gently. "It's me. Thank God you're all right."

I raised my head to try to look past him. "Where's Robert?"

"Robert?" He took a step back. "You want Robert?"

"No, no, no." I reached out for Jim. "No way. But he was here ... maybe yesterday ... he was here. Right here in this room." Panic spread through me and my nerves jangled. My fingernails dug into Jim's arm. "He was here!" My eyes filled with tears and waves of fear coursed through me from my head to my stomach like a bad adrenaline rush.

Jim put his arms around me. I held him tightly, never wanting to let him go. "It's okay. He's not here." He kissed my forehead. "I'll ask the nurse if you're ready to come home."

"Home?"

"With me? Remember? We were going to be together?"

Relief and joy must have shown all over my face. My smile was wide. "Yes." I started climbing out of bed.

"Wait here," Jim said. "I'll ask the nurse if you can leave and she can help you get dressed."

I stuck one leg out of the bed. "Never mind that. I have to get out of here." I looked around. "My clothes ... I ... er...."

Jim pushed me gently back into the bed. "I bought you a couple of things to wear." He pointed to a bag on the chair. "Some sweats and a T-shirt, hoodie, sandals. Just until we get you home and you can go shopping."

You bought me clothes? "How did you know...? When?"

"I came to see you yesterday but they said you'd been sedated."

"Oh, yeah, that's right. Just after the police constable was here, they gave me a shot of something."

"Anyway, so I told them I'd be back. The nurse mentioned you didn't have any wearable clothes. I'll go get her now."

I reached for Jim's hand and swallowed a lump in my throat. "Don't forget to come back." I heard the fear in my voice and hoped it didn't turn him off. Maybe he'd run if he thought he was taking on a basket case. "I can't wait to get out of here," I added.

The nurse who came to help me dress was not Margaret, but she was young and friendly. "My gosh," she said. "Your brother is sure a good-looking fellow."

"My brother?"

"The fellow who just left." She waved towards the door. "And your husband is very handsome too."

I froze with my arms partway through the T-shirt sleeves.

She helped pull the shirt over my head. "Did I say something wrong?"

My mouth was dry and I could hardly swallow. "Is my husband around?"

"Not right now, but the other nurses were talking." She giggled a bit, looking embarrassed. The jerk probably flirted with them. "Do you want me to call him?"

"NO! No, please don't. I-I ran away from him and I won't go back. If he comes ... well, I'm just not going with him." I watched the nurse's eyes widen and her mouth form an "O."

"Oh. Well, now that's good to know. Just so we don't send you off with the wrong person. So will you be going with your brother then?"

"Er, yes, with that man that was just here. Yes. Definitely not with my husband." I began to tremble and my stomach clenched as I remembered what he was capable of. What if he tried to stop us?

The nurse pulled the sweat pants over my legs and as I stood and pulled them up, my ankle felt like a pincushion. The nurse caught me but I pushed her away and hopped to the bathroom dragging my bad foot. I made it just in time before my stomach gave over into the toilet. My hands shook as I tried to turn on the tap to rinse my mouth. The nurse had followed me in and helped me clean up.

"Your husband must have done some terrible things to frighten you like that."

"You have no idea!"

As we came out of the bathroom, Jim was back. "All set?" he asked, nodding thanks to the nurse.

"I'll get you a wheelchair. I know you'd be okay with the crutches, but ... hospital regulations."

As soon as the nurse left, I grabbed a crutch. "Let's get out of here, fast. Never mind the wheelchair."

Jim held me up on my good side while I used the crutch on the other. "It's so good to see you, Andrea." He pulled me close as he guided me down the hall. "It'll be just you and me now. No one's going to hurt you again."

Robert strode around the corner, yelling, "Get your paws off my wife!"

I let out a shriek and turned to try to run. Jim caught me as my crutch clattered to the floor.

"Go away!" I screeched at Robert. Jim had his arms around me, holding me up. He didn't have a chance and took the punch right in his face. The lenses of his smashed glasses skittered on the floor. The glass crunched as Robert's foot stomped on them. Jim fell backwards. I lost my balance and fell almost on top of him, but I wasn't down for long. Robert caught hold of my flailing arm and yanked me up. My sprained ankle sent arrows of pain shooting up my leg.

"Let go of me!" I punched at him but he didn't seem to feel a thing. His huge body was hard as rock. He was dragging me along the hall.

A nurse yelled out, "Call Security."

"Done! They're on their way."

Jim jumped up and landed a punch on Robert's ear.

"You fuckin' son-of-a-bitch," Robert yelled. He shoved me away and I scrabbled along the floor trying to protect my ankle as I fell again. Robert wound up his arm to throw another punch, but Jim was quicker and landed a jab on Robert's nose.

As Robert staggered backwards momentarily, Jim said, "If you don't leave right now, I'll call the cops and tell them how you tried to kill Andrea."

"What the hell are you talking about?"

"The cabin. You burned it down with her locked inside."

"Vandalism! I told you." Robert wiped blood off his nose with his sleeve. His eyes had that glazed over wide-open look they always had when he beat me.

"Back off or you're heading for jail."

Robert came at Jim with his shoulders up, but stopped short—a bear doing a bluff charge—and stayed out of reach of Jim's fists. As the Security guards approached, Robert snarled at me. "You're mine." He hurried down the hall, away from the guards. Then turning back to Jim he growled, "You're going to regret this."

The nurse helped settle me in the wheelchair in the hall. "Good Lord, what a ruckus!" she said. "Is your ankle okay?"

I nodded and she motioned for Jim to take a seat in a nearby corner. She cleaned up his face, put something on the cut, and smoothed a Band-Aid under his eye. "You were lucky that glass only scraped your cheek. It could have been much worse. You should have waited for the wheelchair for Andrea."

"I know, I know." Jim squirmed as he looked at the floor and then sideways at me. "Won't happen again." He got up and we both thanked the nurse.

"Get some crutches at the medical supply store downstairs. The ones you have are only for use in the hospital. They'll give you directions at the nurses' station." She let out a sigh. "And try to keep out of trouble."

Let's get out of here," I muttered to Jim. I stood up and fitted the new crutches under my arms. "Where to?"

Jim pointed to the right side of the parking lot. "This way. Same truck you drove a year ago in the spring."

"Right. When you burnt your face with the molten zinc." I stopped short. "Oh wait! You couldn't drive the boat or the truck then because of your eye. How are you going to drive the truck now without your glasses?"

"Don't worry. I always carry a spare pair of glasses in the truck."

I sighed, remembering better days. "Back then, I had such a wonderful time," I said. "I'd never driven a truck before, but I got us where we wanted to go. I wish things had turned out differently for us after that weekend."

"You'd be married to me now instead of to that maniac." Jim put an arm around my shoulders. "We can still fix that though—if you want to, that is."

I blinked back tears. My heart was trying to leap out of my ribcage. I swallowed hard, and looked into Jim's face. I saw only kindness and love there. I hoped I wasn't just seeing what I desperately wanted to see. "Are you sure you still want me after all this?"

Jim pulled me close and kissed me on the forehead. "More than anything, and forever," he said. I wondered if he had any idea what he was letting himself in for? He didn't know what Robert was capable of.

16

Chapter 3

As I waited for my runaway wife, the migraine started to throb. Sitting in my truck, watching the hospital entrance, I must have dozed off for a few minutes. I'd been traveling since two days ago, brought the Hawkeye down the coast to Lund to pick up my truck and then spent the next morning driving and catching ferries. Slept in the truck last night—a few minutes at a time. A hospital parking lot in downtown Vancouver wasn't ideal. Stupid to fall asleep just now. I might have missed them. I'd give it five more minutes and if they didn't show I'd go back in and look around.

Hah! There they were, him all huddled over her in case she fell. What a scrawny excuse for a man. The wimp looked stupider than usual without his glasses. Bloody four-eyed freak. *What the hell does she see in him?* Ah, piss on it. She wasn't much use to me until she had two working legs. Let him look after her until she got better. I could always grab her in a few weeks when she was stronger and could do a good day's work around the place. Building a cabin was going to be a bit of a grunt and she could damn well help me. After all, it was her fault the cabin burned down. She shouldn't have made me so mad. She was my wife. It was her job—her duty—to help her husband.

I could have run over and really punched out Jim's lights right then, but she would scream blue murder and that would attract a lot of attention in a place like this. Vancouver was not like Lund where the handful of people who lived there minded their own business. I didn't need trouble from the police, who might still be nearby after the scuffle in the hallway. As Jim and Andrea left the parking lot, I pulled out behind them. Looked like they were heading for the Lion's Gate Bridge. Traffic was pretty heavy, but if I lost sight of them, it wouldn't matter too much. I figured they were most likely going to the Horseshoe Bay ferry terminal. I'd follow and probably I'd see them at the ferry parking lot.

Along the Upper Levels highway, I spotted them. Jim was driving more slowly than the rest of the traffic. He'd be having a bit of trouble seeing, I guessed, and also he wasn't any more used to city traffic than I was. I pulled over into the slow lane three cars behind him. This road only went to the ferry, really. I doubted that they were heading up to the Sunshine Coast—not with Andrea's ankle the way it was. They'd be heading straight for Jim's house. Well, I'd be nearby. Have a bit of fun with them.

The ferry was big enough a person could get lost on it. They'd never know I was on it with them. When we docked at Nanaimo, I'd follow them up island to Comox. Then I could take my time and set up someplace near Jim's house, living in my truck. The swimming pool was a good place to get cleaned up and use the facilities. I'd manage just fine. No need for a motel room.

I would make their life hell. Jim was going to wish he'd never laid eyes on Andrea and one way or another, she would see that she'd made a big mistake leaving me.

Chapter 4

Jim turned down the long driveway to his house. The cedar hedge was overgrown. He hadn't been home all summer so it looked rough, but who cared. It was wonderful just to be here. I remembered Stan, at the haulout place in Lund telling me last year that when Jim's father died, he had left him a beautiful house. The place was as gorgeous as I remembered from my visit over a year ago. Tall fir trees surrounded the property. The house had brown cedar siding that blended in with the smaller trees and shrubs nearby. Little birds flew up out of the high grass and bushes as we drove past.

"Look at all the birds you have out here," I said. "I love birds."

"They like trees and shrubs. Gives them a place to hide if there's a hawk or a cat around."

"But I never saw many birds when I lived in the cabin." An involuntary shudder rippled over me. *I shouldn't have mentioned the cabin, but I can't pretend it didn't happen.*

Jim glanced over at me. "You okay?"

"Fine." *Fine now, with you.*

"Good. Well, the reason you didn't have many birds there is because you probably didn't have much edge effect," Jim said.

"What's that?"

"Open grassy areas with shrubs and plants at the edges so animals can come out into the open and yet be close to cover if they're in danger."

"Guess you're my edge effect."

"How so?"

"I can be out in the open, free, enjoy the sunshine, and if I need help I can run to you—my edge effect."

Jim faked a swipe of his forehead. "Whew! For a second there I thought you meant I was like an old shrub."

I gave him a peck on the cheek. "Silly. But you do have a certain charm when you're a bit scruffy."

Jim parked the truck and reached over for me. His lips were soft and warm on mine. His two-days' growth of beard scratched at my cheek. I scraped at it lightly with my fingernails and growled, "Scruffy."

I hobbled up to the front door and waited while Jim unlocked it. He turned and took my crutches away. "Steady there." He leaned the crutches against the house, picked me up, and carried me over the threshold.

"Oh, this is nice." I leaned my head into his neck. "I feel like a bride."

Jim's lips found mine again and by the way his tongue probed between my teeth, I knew there would be more fun to follow later. I was still tingling when he set me down gently. I waited while he brought the crutches in.

"I want you to feel that this is your house as long as you stay here," he said, "and I hope it will be forever— at least until we both want to move to another place together."

I held onto the doorframe. I needed to hold on, not only because of my ankle but because my heart was thumping so hard. I tried not to grin so unabashedly, but if ever there were sweeter words, I didn't know what they were.

I took a careful step forward and put my arms around Jim. I pulled him close to me. "Thank you. I'd be really happy if things worked out for us." *You have no idea how happy.*

As I took the stairs slowly, and one at a time, Jim had already rushed up them. I had to smile at what sounded like hurried straightening up of the bedroom. By the time I got there, he had shut the closet door and stood in front of it protectively with a pink tinge to his face.

"I'll tidy up properly later on," he said. "Bathroom is in here." I followed him through a door off the bedroom. "You can freshen up." He pulled a facecloth and towel out of the cabinet under the counter and found a spare toothbrush in a drawer. "These are for you to use. Help yourself to anything you need. I'll use the downstairs bathroom."

It felt so good to wash my face. I pulled open one of the drawers and found the toothpaste. On the counter, all the toiletries were men's things, but that would change as soon as I could buy a few items of my own. I didn't even have any face cream, or a fingernail file. Nothing at all. I freshened up from the long trip and hobbled out of the bathroom.

Jim was waiting for me. He pointed at the bed that he had straightened out while I was in the bathroom. "I think you should try it out to see if you'll be comfortable sleeping in it tonight."

"I guess I should...." I hardly had the words out of my mouth when Jim lifted me onto the bed.

"Now don't move. You don't want to hurt your ankle. I'd better take your clothes off for you." He started with the T-shirt, pulling it up over my head. I had no bra yet. I felt exposed and my nipples shivered until Jim's mouth covered them, gently sucking on them one at a time.

I squirmed with pleasure and ran my hands through his hair and down his shoulder blades. "Ooh, that feels so good, what you're doing."

I reached under to unbutton his shirt and fumbled so much Jim stopped to help me. With his shirt off, he looked even more delicious. He wasn't the scrawny guy I thought I remembered from Masset last summer. That had been a hasty lovemaking in the woods back then with most of our clothes on. I liked this better. Much better.

I let my palms glide down his chest. "You look like a panther," I told him.

Jim smiled, unzipped his pants, and then hesitated. He pulled my sweats and panties down in one motion, maneuvering them carefully over the sore ankle. His hands were everywhere, exploring and stroking me, stopping only long enough to help his feet kick his jeans to the floor.

I reached up my arms to him. As he lay down on top of me, propping himself up on his elbows, I could feel his erection. Soft and hard at the same time. I felt faint when I realized what a treasure I had found. "Never mind the preliminaries. Just put it in me."

"I will. Don't worry. I will." He lay down sideways up against me and his hand wandered over my mound where his fingers explored the depths. "But not just yet."

"Oh, come on." I arched my back, pushing myself towards him.

Jim buried his face in my neck, nibbling at a place under my ear that sent goosebumps all over me, while his fingers pushed deeper and slid over sensitive spots on their way out. The itch was unbearable.

"Jim!" I clasped him to myself. "I need it now."

"Me too," he breathed in my ear.

I pulled his bottom closer and writhed, trying to make contact with that substantial penis that he was working so hard to withhold. "Ouch!"

He pulled away. "What?"

"Never mind. Just my ankle. For God's sake will you just put it in?"

He chuckled. "Oh, you want something I have?"

I pounded on his chest with one fist. "Dammit!"

And then the sensation of that wonderful male part filling me up, sent me into wave after wave of ecstasy. I closed my eyes and the panther was loving me, setting every cell in my body on fire. I couldn't get enough and it seemed that the panther was taking over, riding me like an animal made purely of muscle and sinew. His gentle thrusts came deeper and faster like our breathing and gasping and clutching. "Own me, own me," I thought. "I want to be yours, forever."

The panther filled me up with one final thrust and a growl, and collapsed onto me. "That's good."

I let out a long sigh and let my arms and legs relax. "Yeah, it was."

"No, I mean yes, it was, but I meant, it's good that you want to be mine forever."

Oh shit. "Did I say that out loud?"

"Involuntary confession, I guess." Jim grinned and kissed my cheek. "But don't worry. Your secret is safe with me.

"Why don't we have a shower together? I can help you. Then I'll get something out of the freezer for our supper? Pizza okay?"

"Pizza?" I couldn't remember when I'd last had a pizza. "I'd love to have pizza." We had a long shower, needing the extra time to deal with Jim's erection—again. I was happy to help him take care of it.

He slipped out of the shower then. I sat on the bench at one end of the shower stall and shampooed my hair.

"I'll pour us some wine for when you get out of the shower."

A few minutes later, I stepped out to find that Jim had gathered a few things and put them in the bathroom for me to wear: a soft cream-coloured cotton shirt and a pair of blue Joe Boxer lounge pants.

"Put these on for now. We'll get some clothes for you tomorrow."

With tear-filled eyes, I reached for Jim and drew him close. "Thank you so much. No one has been this good to me in a long time."

"I love you, Andrea. It's easy to be good to you."

I wiped at my eyes. "I love you too, Jim."

Early the next morning, I asked Jim if he would mind if I used his phone. I had an important call to make.

"Hi, Mom? It's Andrea."

"Andrea? Oh thank the Lord. Are you all right? We've been so worried about you. Haven't heard a thing for so long and your last letters sounded absolutely miserable. How *are* you?"

At the sound of her voice, my throat closed up. It hurt like hell and I couldn't undo the knot that kept me from speaking.

"Andrea? Are you there?" She sounded worried now. I had to find my voice and let her know I was okay. After all, that was the main reason for phoning. I managed to get a little sound out.

"M-hmm. I...." A big sniff escaped me. I gasped for breath. "I'm here." Another gulp for air. "I'm fine. Now."

"Where are you calling from?"

"Jim's house. I'm at Jim's. I finally got away from Robert—it was terrible."

"Oh, Andrea, honey. I'm so sorry. But it's good that you're with Jim. I always knew there was something there."

"Yes, he's been very good to me. I'll be fine now."

"I'm so glad to hear it. Give me Jim's phone number before I forget."

I could hear her scrambling for a pen. "Where's Dad?" I asked.

"At work."

"I forgot it was later in Ontario. Tell him I said hello and I love him." My throat closed again. "And Cheryl too. Tell my sister I love her."

"I will. But what about you? Do you need anything, dear?"

I had to smile in spite of the emotional nostalgia. "Yes, you might say that. But that's not why I called. I have nothing. Absolutely nothing. But I'm free again. I'll talk to you more next time. Can you give me your email address? I have Internet access now. I can write you a lot of the stuff rather than waste your time."

"Nonsense. I love hearing your voice, and I'm so glad you called. We must not lose touch again."

She gave me her e-mail address and I gave her Jim's phone number. I assured her I was fine, that she needn't worry, and I reminded her not to send any more letters to the Squirrel Cove Post Office. "Love you, Mom."

"Love you too, Andrea. I'll talk to you soon."

At about ten, Jim's long-time friend Giselle appeared at the door with a big garbage bag. She dropped the bag and put her arms around me. "I'm so happy you're here. Jim told me a bit about what you've been going through."

I nodded and grimaced. "A lot of water's gone under the bridge since we were at your party last year."

Giselle glanced over at Jim as she picked up the garbage bag again. She took my hand and headed for the bedroom. "Excuse us, Jim. We have some clothes to try on."

"What...?" I had no choice but to follow Giselle.

Clothes poured out of the bag as she dumped it out on the bed. "Jim phoned me from the hospital yesterday morning and asked if I had anything for you to wear until you can go shopping for your own clothes. Come on. Let's try some things on. I'll help you with your ankle." She looked at me appraisingly. "I think you'll easily fit into these jeans that are too tight for me."

"Giselle! This is so good of you. I have absolutely no clothes. Nothing. And now I feel like I just won the lottery." I slipped off the Joe Boxers and sat on the bed. Giselle pulled the jeans over my sprained ankle. Then I stuffed my good foot into the other pant leg. Standing, I pulled the jeans up easily. "It's like they were made for me."

"They're yours," Giselle announced happily. She rummaged through the pile and found a lightweight shirt that suited me perfectly. "And now," she said, "you're coming to town with me. I made a hair appointment for you, and we'll get a manicure and pedicure and the whole nine yards. You can sit down the whole time. No need to walk on your bad ankle."

My smile disappeared. "But I can't!"

"Why not? Of course you can."

"I have no money."

"Don't worry. This is Jim's treat."

Jim waved goodbye to us as we pulled out of the driveway. I turned my face to the window and blinked more tears away. Seemed as if all I could do is cry these days, but they were happy tears. Not those hopeless tears of despair and loneliness I shed when I lived with that monster in a cabin in the middle of nowhere. It would take me a while to get used to people being nice to me again.

"I feel so completely ... humbled—yeah, I guess that's the word—having to ask for the basic things most people take for granted. I've always had a job, my own money, a bank account, a driver's licence. But when I was living with Robert, all that disappeared. He even closed my bank account. It tied me to him more securely if I had no means of getting money to travel."

"And you were way up the coast, in the bush," Giselle said. "No chance to do anything."

"When he set fire to the cabin, I knew I had to get away or he would kill me. But there was no time to pack my things. Here I am now with not even a hairbrush or a dime to my name. It's not what I'm used to. I was always independent, not relying on others for favours."

"You'll get back on track. It will take a bit of time and some help from your friends, but that's what friends are for."

"I know, and you've been so good to me, Giselle. I just hope I can do something for you one day."

Giselle pulled over to the curb and parked in front of a shop. "First stop, the hairdresser's." I was thankful for Giselle's steady babble. Gave me time to pull myself together. "I hope you don't mind me choosing my favourite hairdresser for your appointment. I figured you could use a trim. Don't suppose you've had much chance to have a nice haircut for a while."

I must look like a ragamuffin. All that time without a proper haircut. Without pampering of any kind at all. "Does it show?" I joked. "I think the last haircut I got was just before I got married last fall. It seems like so much longer. That one year of marriage felt more like ten. I thought I'd never be able to get away. It's all I thought about. Getting away."

"That Robert sounds like a real bastard."

I shivered at the sound of his name. "I'll never go back to him. Never. Even if I have to kill myself first."

Giselle patted my arm and slowly shook her head. "Jim would never let that happen. You're safe with him.

"I'll come in with you now and introduce you to my hairdresser."

Look at you!" Giselle stood back grinning at me as I came out of the salon. "Andrea, you look *magnifique*."

I gave her a nudge and looked at the ground. "Oh, go on. So what's next?"

"We can go clothes shopping another day when your ankle is better, but let's get you some underwear for now. Start from the ground up. Right? I know just the shop."

We got in Giselle's car and as I turned to buckle up my seat belt, I was face to face with Robert. It couldn't be him. But it was! He was standing just outside the car. I shrieked, and slapped the button down to lock the car. "Go, Giselle. Go! GO!"

Chapter 5

Late last night, I cruised the street Jim lived on. *I choke on his name. Traitor! We were best buddies!* It was getting dark so I found a place to park for the night near the mailbox turnaround area at the end of his block. I walked up his road to check out his house and yard. With plenty of time and the cover of darkness, all those trees and shrubs were perfect screens. I could stand behind the tall firs for hours and no one would even know I was there. Lights on in the house. Like watching a movie.

The fun went out of it though when Andrea—MY wife—snuggled up to that bastard. Pissed me off. I had to do my anger management gimmicks that the psychiatrist taught me, pounding my fist into my hand and saying some swear word. After I calmed down I wondered why seeing her bothered me so much. If I was honest with myself, I guess I still loved her. Sure she'd misbehaved and needed to be punished—plenty of time for that—but I did love her. She was the only woman who was kind to me beyond a first date. She understood me. She knew when to leave me alone, when to be a companion. She helped darken the room and kept quiet when I had those horrible headaches. She was good for sex.

Yeah, I wanted her back. Wouldn't be easy. She didn't seem to want to come on her own. His fault. He was brainwashing her. Playing nice. Telling her lies about me. My best friend. Traitor! Bastard! I trusted him. Well, I'd get him.

This morning I sat near the mailbox and waited. There weren't many houses on Jim's street, so I could watch the comings and goings. Not that there was much happening. It was a quiet street. I had nothing but time, so I waited, read a paper I filched from the box beside the group mailboxes. Eventually something would happen.

What was this? A little white car went up the street and turned into Jim's driveway. Some woman with short, dark, curly hair and big sunglasses was driving. I sat tight and waited for her to come back out. I'd follow her and find out who his friends were. That didn't take long. Twenty minutes and she was out again. Hot damn! It was my lucky day. She had Andrea with her. I was ready for them. They didn't even notice me. I pulled out and let the truck crawl along for a while—put some space between us.

Down the little country road and into town, I followed them and watched them park on the main street. I pulled into the mall parking lot nearby. Andrea got out and stood with her weight on one leg while she bent over to get the crutches out of the back. *Nice ass! She's still got what it takes to get me hard.* I slouched down in the truck in case she happened to look over my way. Over the dash I could see her going across the street with the other woman. *Ahhh! Into the hairdresser's.* So she was getting her hair done. The other woman came back out. I figured Andrea might be a while.

I got out and stretched my legs. They were a bit cramped up from sleeping in the back of the truck, but I'd have to get used to it. It was a makeshift camperizing job—just a mattress and a couple of boxes to store things. Not all that comfortable but a few hardships weren't going to hurt me. Be worth it when I put my plan into effect. I didn't expect to get Andrea to come willingly, but sooner or later I'd have the chance to grab her. After all, she was my wife. *Is* my wife! I strolled past the beauty salon. Out of the corner of my eye I could see her with her head in the sink, legs spread apart just wide enough for me to slip in there. *Wishful thinking. I gotta get a grip.*

Back in the truck I slid down in the seat and pulled my cap low over my forehead. If anyone wondered what I was doing it would look as if I was having a snooze.

A little over an hour later, I saw her coming out the salon door. I hurried to get out. Had to get over there before they took off. I walked up the sidewalk coming up from behind them. The other woman saw me but to her I was just another person on the street. She didn't know who I was. Why would she? But Andrea would, if she looked back. I waited 'til she was getting into the car.

"Andrea!" I called. "Wait up. I just want to talk." I hardly got the words out when she slammed her fist onto the door lock and screamed. I spun around before I attracted the driver's attention and disappeared between a couple of parked cars.

That didn't go so well. My heart was still hammering to jump out of my chest. Shit! Maybe I missed this time, but she hadn't seen the last of me yet. I had my bed in the truck and a credit card in my pocket. I was good for a while. I'd be watching her and watching for my chance. Had to show her she couldn't do this to me.

Chapter 6

Giselle's eyes widened and she gasped. "What's wrong? Are you hurt? What happened?"

I flapped my hand at her. "Just drive. Go! Please! Go! Hurry."

As she pulled away from the curb, I turned to search for any sign of Robert. A few people walked along the sidewalk, some cutting across the mall parking lot presumably back to their cars. Could Robert have been parked there, watching for me? I scanned the vehicles, but saw no sign of him. Nothing. He had disappeared. I was sure I hadn't imagined him. He was real. I saw him. Didn't I? What if I was losing my mind? A wave of fear and despair swept over me. I let my face drop into my hands and sobbed.

Giselle pulled out and turned left. Down the street at the marina park she pulled over in the nearly empty parking lot. She shut off the engine and put an arm on my shoulder.

"What happened, Andrea?" She rubbed my back and I felt myself relax. "Tell me. What is it?"

I took a deep quavery breath. "Robert. He was there."

"Aw, no. That can't be." Giselle shook her head. "He can't be here. You must still be upset from all you went through."

"No. I saw him. He spoke to me!" I choked back another sob and patted my pockets looking for a Kleenex. *Oh God! She thinks I'm delusional Maybe she's right. Maybe I'm as crazy as Robert.* "Really, Giselle. Believe me!"

"Here." Giselle handed me a tissue and took a deep breath as if she was praying for patience. "Okay, where did you see him?"

"He was right beside the car when I reached to close the door."

"And you didn't see him when you were still on the sidewalk?"

"I know that doesn't make sense, but no. He came out of nowhere." I thought for a moment. "I leaned in to put my crutches in the back and when I sat down and closed the door, he was right there."

"You said he talked to you. What did he say?"

"He said my name. Said he just wanted to talk to me. I slammed the door shut and locked it."

Giselle was shaking her head as she started the car. I knew she didn't believe me.

"Look, Giselle, I appreciate you taking me out to get my hair done and all that, but I think it's probably best if you just take me home—well, back to Jim's."

"You can't let this guy control you like that." She reached over and patted my hand. "Come on. I'll watch out for you. He can't do anything while we're together and in town. Too many people around."

I scrunched up my face trying not to cry, and sucked in air through my clenched teeth, trying to pull myself together. Giselle was right. Wasn't that what I told Monique when she came to see me at the hospital? I would never let any man hurt me again. I blew my nose and wiped my wet cheeks with my hands. Took a deep breath. "You're right. He's probably gone and anyway, what can he do?" I shuddered remembering exactly what he could do. I put my shoulders back. "Let's go then." I forced myself to smile.

"Aw … right!" Giselle cheered and held up a hand to high-five me.

I bought some sexy underwear at Giselle's favourite lingerie shop. I was a bit on the thin side after my year with Robert and then my ordeal of walking through miles of rough terrain, trying to escape him. It wouldn't hurt to have one or two pretty pairs of panties, besides the sensible cotton ones, to help make me look more appealing to Jim.

With the underwear taken care of, we went to a couple of small boutiques in town. The clothes were beautiful. "Oh my God," I whispered.

"Nice things, eh?"

"Too nice."

"Why? What's wrong?"

"I can't shop here." I put the soft lavender blouse back on the rack. "Did you see the prices?"

"Never mind that." Giselle picked up the blouse I'd had my eye on. "Jim said you were to get at least two good outfits. He won't want you to come home with junk. Besides you have lots of casual stuff in that bag of hand-me-downs I brought you."

"But it's so expensive." *And it's not my money.*

"Don't worry about that. Jim can afford it. And he'll be happy when he sees you looking good again. Quality clothes make you feel good too." She flipped through the racks and pulled out a pair of red jeans and a flowing white blouse. "Try these on while I find some black pants to go with your lavender blouse."

And so Giselle outfitted me with the basics of a new wardrobe. I tried to pick up the bags but with my crutches I couldn't manage it. Giselle took over.

"Here. Let me do it. It's no problem." She was loaded down with bags of new clothes as I limped out of the store. Shuffling the bags around, she groped for her car keys and opened the door for me. I hated that she was putting herself out for me. I didn't like being a burden on anyone. It was time to be more independent, the way I was when I first came out here from Ontario a year and a half ago.

As we got into the downtown traffic, I noted the names on signs and shop windows to familiarize myself with town. Across the street and half a block down from the clothing store a man got up from the bench he'd been sitting on. Robert again! I gasped. He waved to me and pointed to his eyes and then at me. "I'm watching you," his gesture said.

Giselle noticed my sharp intake of breath. "You okay?" She glanced at the road and then at me again. "You're white. Look like you saw a ghost."

I tried to keep my chin from quivering. "I did," I whispered.

Chapter 7

I almost didn't recognize Andrea when she hobbled through the doorway in her red jeans and white blouse. I had to make a conscious effort to close my mouth. Fashion model gorgeous, only not that tall. Her rich chestnut brown hair curled down her back past her shoulders. It was shorter, but it looked good. It reminded me of the day she and Monique were helping me on my boat, making sure I made it to Comox. I shuddered remembering the molten zinc burns around my eye. I couldn't see well then, but I could smell her just fine. Then, when I'd held her and put my cheek next to her hair, I inhaled flowers and fresh sea air. I didn't know it at the time, but I was already falling in love with her.

"Andrea! Wow! You look gorgeous!" I leaned her crutches on the wall and took her in my arms. Then I stepped back to have a better look. "Nice outfit. What else did you buy?"

I motioned for Giselle to come in, but she shook her head. She set the bags down on the floor in the entry and handed me my debit card. "I'll be going now. Got some things to do. See you later, Andrea. That was fun."

Andrea turned to look at Giselle. "Thanks so much, Giselle. For ... for everything."

"No problem." As Andrea navigated the stairs to the living room, Giselle made a quick "call me" motion with her hand.

Now what could that be about?

Cup of coffee?" I asked. "Or did you stop for lunch? Are you hungry?"

"Yes, no, and not right now." She sat on the couch picking at her thumbnail.

In the kitchen I put on a pot of coffee and thawed some frozen blueberry muffins in the microwave. I glanced over at her. She was staring at her hands, still picking away nervously.

I sat down on the couch next to her and took her hands in mine. "What's wrong?"

Her eyes brimmed with tears and I expected to hear bad news. She didn't want to stay with me after all. She'd decided to go back to her folks in Ontario. She needed to get her head together. She was going back to live with Monique. My heart was sinking down to my feet. "What?" I whispered, my hands tightening on hers.

Her fingers trembled. "He's here." She squeezed the words out. "Robert is here. In Comox."

No way. Oh man, maybe I've hooked up with a nutcase. I shook my head. "Why do you think he's here? Why would he come here when he has nowhere to live? No friends, no house." She was biting her lips, her face contorted, trying not to cry. Tore me up to see her like this. "Aw, Andrea. Come here." I pulled her close to me and felt her body quivering every few seconds. "He's not here, and even if he was, you're safe with me. I won't let him hurt you."

She pressed her head into my chest. "I'm so scared."

"Don't be. You're safe." I kissed her forehead. Her soft violet eyes brimmed with tears. "What makes you think he's here anyway?"

"I saw him! He spoke to me! I locked the car door just in time." She shuddered. "That was in Comox. Then when we were in Courtenay, he was on the sidewalk on a bench. He waved to me and did this." She showed me the "I'm watching you" gesture.

"What does Giselle think?"

She shrugged her shoulders. "She didn't see him. She thinks it's all in my head."

I didn't say, "So do I," but I was thinking it. No way Robert was over here, but it would take some time for Andrea to get over her paranoia. "Coffee's ready. Look, Andrea, how about if we get our minds off Robert? Let's go out to dinner tonight. We could make it an early dinner and a movie."

She nodded and forced a smile that didn't reach her terrified eyes. I was sick with worry over her. She was way more of a mess than I originally thought. Shit. This was getting too complicated. *Yes, I love her, but Jesus, what am I letting myself in for? On the other hand, I've seen how crazy Robert can be. What if he really is here and goes nuts?*

We had dinner at Tiny's Restaurant, not too far from the movie theater. I knew the food was good, but I'd never noticed before how basic the ambience was.

I felt the bench I was sitting on. The cheap Naugahyde covering had barely any stuffing under it. "I haven't been here for a while. I didn't remember the seats being so hard."

Sitting across from me in the booth, Andrea smiled at me. "That's okay. It's close to the theater, so it's practical."

Just like her to think about being practical, but I should have brought her to a nicer restaurant. She's way too pretty and delicate for a place like this.

"I remember that you were very practical when we worked on the Serenity last year. After I splashed molten zinc on myself, I was going to try to keep working with my wrist in a bandage and a patch over my eye. You were so sensible, making me go lie down while you and Stan finished the copper painting and put the cooling pipes back on. If I'd kept on working, I might have gotten an infection in that wrist and been off work a lot longer."

"Seemed like a no-brainer to me. You needed to go lie down. Besides, I got to know Stan a bit better and we worked well together. I learned lots from working with him, and I was happy to do it for you."

She was so sweet. "Still, practical or not, another time we'll go someplace fancy." *For sure she deserved better.*

She smiled across the table at me with those beautiful eyes. Seeing her look so innocent and vulnerable, I wanted to protect her and love her forever. Could I hang onto her that long? What if she was unstable though, seeing things that weren't there? Imagining being stalked. But I loved her. Really loved her. I shouldn't have doubted her. Andrea's smile was encouraging and I looked down while I swallowed a lump in my throat and blinked away the mist collecting in my eyes. How did she manage to put on a happy face and wear those battle scars at the same time? Her left cheek had a slight greenish tinge just under the eye and her forehead was criss-crossed with tiny scabs from a gravel burn she got while she was trying to escape from Robert. She was fragile and yet there was something tough inside her that made her run for her life through the bush. She had to have suffered terribly to make a run for it like that. She can't be crazy if she survived and had the guts to run away. Most women—hell, most men—wouldn't risk going through those woods, unprepared, knowing there were bears, cougars, and wolves out there.

It must have been a terrifying situation for her, living with Robert. Such a big man, and so out of control. *Ha! That's funny. Him being out of control when he's such a control freak about everything except his own behaviour.*

"Cast iron, and frail," I mumbled.

"What's that?"

"Oh, just some lyrics of Joni Mitchell's. You know that song, 'Shades of Scarlet Conquering'?" She shook her head. "I'll play it for you sometime. About a woman who is tough and yet breakable at the same time. Like you, at least in that part of the song."

She bit her lip, worried again. "Is that how I seem to you?"

I put my hand over hers. "I know you're strong, but … I want to protect you."

Her smile widened and she leaned her head to the side. "Thanks," she whispered. "That's really sweet of you."

We picked up the menus and studied them. Seconds later, I looked over my menu at her. Yes, she was still there. "I still can't believe you're really here with me. Finally."

"I hope you won't find my baggage too much to bear," she said.

"What do you mean?"

"Well, today I realized that it's not going to be so simple to live with you."

Alarms bells rang somewhere inside my stomach. "Something wrong?"

She looked away and sucked in her breath between gritted teeth. "What if Robert keeps on following me everywhere I go in town? What if he grabs me and makes me come with him?" She pulled her hands down to her lap, but I had seen them trembling.

An exasperated sigh escaped me. "Andrea, you've got to stop worrying about him. Look, if it makes you feel better, I'll go with you whenever you leave our place. If you go grocery shopping or when you buy more clothes, I'll go with you. Okay?"

She nodded, but her brow was furrowed. If I got my hands on that bastard, I'd kill him, even if he was a lot bigger than me. "Come on. Forget about him and let's order. What would you like?"

After the waitress took our order I excused myself to run to the men's room. From there, I could make a quick call to Giselle.

Walking back to the truck after the movie in the growing darkness, I thought Andrea was quieter than usual. "How's your ankle?"

"A bit sore right now. Must be from sitting for two hours." She winced as she limped along. "It'll get better once I get moving again."

"Hold onto my arm and don't put too much weight on your ankle. We're almost there." Seconds later I opened the truck door and helped her inside.

We'd been driving for a good five minutes and she hadn't said much. "Kind of sad, wasn't it?" I said.

"Huh?" She gave her eyes a quick wipe with the back of her hand before turning to look at me.

"The movie. Kind of sad that he missed out. The girl had given up on him. I guess she thought he was lost forever after his plane crashed."

"Yeah. He probably thought he was too, stuck on that island all alone."

I reached for her hand. "Oh no.... Andrea ... I—"

She patted my hand with hers. "That's okay. You didn't know it was going to be so much like what I just went through."

"We shouldn't have come to—"

"Of course we should. I can't hide from real life forever."

A realistic attitude was all very well, and I liked to think of myself as a realist, but Andrea had only recently come out of a traumatic situation and I had just shoved her nose right back into it, making her remember it. *What an idiot I am!* My whole body seemed to sag together. I felt like such a thoughtless clod.

"But it must have been awful seeing yourself in his situation. I should never have brought you to this movie. It was like making you relive the whole thing. I'm so sorry. I don't know what I was thinking ... well, I wasn't. I should have checked out what 'Castaway' was about first."

"Look at it this way, Jim. At least we're together. We didn't lose each other like Tom Hanks and Téa Leoni in the movie." Her hand crept over to my thigh and I curled my fingers around it, brought it up to my lips and kissed it.

I reached over and caressed the back of her head. "That's right. We're together and that's how I hope we'll stay. Just forget all about Robert and that other life. It's in the past. Over and done." I preferred to believe Giselle over Andrea on this one. When I called her earlier she said she thought Andrea was paranoid and seeing Robert when he wasn't really there. *No way he'd come over here to hound her. Would he?*

Arriving at home, I thought the house looked awfully dark. "That's funny. I'm sure I left the porch lights and the foyer lights on when we left." I fumbled trying to find the keyhole to unlock the door. Inside I turned on the entry light in the pitch dark house.

"It's so good to come home to your house, Jim. Like a safe haven. I want to pinch myself to make sure I'm not dreaming. Part of me keeps expecting to be back in that cabin with Robert, waiting for the next blow up." Andrea sounded like she was trying to look for the positive but her smile was trembling.

I hated to see her like this, but I was going to get her through it. I took her by the elbow. "Here, let's get you up these stairs and into the living room. I seem to remember that you liked brandy when you were here ... gosh ... almost two years ago."

"Yes, I did like the brandy. And the company. Back then you were the one with the injury. Remember? With that patch over your eye?"

I got the brandy glasses out and brought the bottle into the living room. "I needed the medicinal benefits badly then." I smiled, remembering how badly I'd wanted to get into her pants and she held me off, saying she didn't know me well enough. "Here you go." I added a little extra to her glass as I thought she needed to relax.

"I think this time we can have a brandy without worrying about your eye."

"Chin-chin. Here's to my two good eyes and soon to your two good legs." We clinked glasses and I looked around the room, showing off my two good eyes. "I can see perfectly. And I see perfection." I leaned over and gave her a kiss. "Nice flowers, by the way."

"What flowers?"

"In the pot on the end table. Didn't you buy them when you were shopping today?" I shrugged. "Maybe Giselle left them and I only just noticed them. Don't know what they are, but they're nice."

Andrea's glass slipped out of her hand and landed clumsily on the table, spilling half the brandy. "No! No, I didn't bring them." She spoke in a tight voice. "Neither did Giselle."

All the colour had drained out of her face.

"They're … they're … orchids," she whispered, and grabbed my arm. "Jim! He's been in your house." Her fingers clenched into a claw and her eyes grew round and wide. "He might still be here!" She choked out the words. "What are we going to do? Wh- what if he's hiding in a closet?"

Shit! She's really a paranoid mess. We've got to get a handle on this. "Sh-sh-sh! It's okay. He wouldn't be that stupid to be in the house. And anyway, what makes you think Robert brought the orchids?"

"Because that's what he did to convince me to marry him. Brought me expensive orchids." She gasped for breath between sobs. "And he brought some to the hospital too."

"Maybe it was one of Giselle's friends saying welcome."

"No, I know—"

"Look, tomorrow I'll phone Giselle and clear this up. For tonight, I'll check every room and every closet so you don't have to worry. Okay?"

Andrea nodded ever so slightly. She looked so defeated, still banged up from her ordeal, and now this. I'd had no idea how weak she was mentally. I had to get that creep out of her life.

Chapter 8

Lying down in the camperized back of my truck, I reminisced about my day. I wished I could have been a fly on the wall when that jerk and my wife got home from the movie. I would have loved that scene, her all freaked out, and him all a-fluster.

I had followed them across town to the restaurant and then the movie theater, always being careful to keep my distance, even though neither of them knew I had a truck. They stood in the lineup for the movie outside the theater, Andrea looking smart in her red jeans. She had a nice tight ass and didn't seem to be aware of the heads she turned. Suits me. But they had no business looking at her ass, and if she had responded it would have pissed me off. As it was, it pissed me off that Jim would let her go out dressed like that. He was so stupid. Didn't he know men would gawk at her? What was he thinking? I had to get her back and get her under control again. This liberal shit wasn't doing her any good.

I could have left once they were in the line, but I had plenty of time and a good vantage point from the parking lot, and mainly, I wanted to be sure they went in. As soon as Jim put his money down, I was out of there.

I took it easy, driving along the road by Comox Bay, enjoying the scenery at the estuary. It was quiet and I pulled in to the parking lot of the bird viewing area. It had a gazebo, empty now, where birdwatchers could get out of the rain while they glassed the marshes or took photographs. I was there to do neither, but after hanging out in a parking lot at the movie theater and restaurant for an hour, I'd felt the headache coming on. I was ready for some quiet time.

When my brother and I were little, I could count on the headache every time my drunken bitch of a mother slapped us around. As soon as she passed out, I'd go to the forest to get out of the house. The silence there soothed my pounding head.

The bench in the gazebo overlooking the Comox Estuary gave me almost the same feeling of relief. I listened to the sounds of the marsh. Ducks dabbled near the edges among the reeds, softly gabbling in duck conversations. A great blue heron stood along the far side of the tidal backwater, still as a statue. I watched him move cautiously, a long time between motions. If you weren't paying attention you'd swear he never moved at all, but that was how he moved in for the kill. That would be me, stalking Andrea. One move, then nothing for a while. When she felt reassured that all was well, I'd make another move. She'd be more rattled with every event, until I had her terrified again, just the way she used to be when we were together in the cabin—the way she would be again one day.

It took about half an hour but my headache faded at last. I drove on towards Jim's place just out of town. I still had work to do tonight.

I parked by the mailbox again and walked up Jim's road. Even though it was still light out, there were enough bushes around Jim's house that I didn't worry about being seen. Besides the place was semi-rural and it wasn't as if there were other houses close by.

The upstairs push-out window was open and it was no big deal to grab the stepladder lying beside the woodshed, get up on the hip of the first floor roof, and walk up it to the second floor level. I stepped in as easily as going through the front door.

I wished I could have seen her face when she saw the little potted orchid I had picked up from Home Depot. Her eyes would get huge and she'd remember me. Oh yes, she'd know it was me. She would have seen it by now and she'd know I was not giving up. Nobody was going to have the last laugh on me. She knew I was coming after her. And when I got her, I'd teach her she'd better not try leaving me ever again.

But first I was going to have some fun with her. Unnerve her. Punish her. Next time would be even easier. I would go through the front door or any door I chose. It had been easy to find a spare house key in the rack where Jim kept all his keys. I'd have a copy made and return the original next time. From now on I'd come and go as I pleased.

Chapter 9

Jim did everything to try to make me feel safe. He checked every closet—and there were a lot of them. He even checked the laundry chute and the garage and under the stairs.

"All clear," he said. "Now, you're safe with me and I don't want you to worry. The doors are locked and it's just us inside."

"Just to be sure I'll put my bear spray in the night table drawer," I said. "In case you're not here sometime and I need it."

I hadn't thought about Jim feeling as if I didn't trust in his protection. He looked a bit disappointed at first, but then he agreed. "Sure, why not? It can't hurt."

I put my hands on his arms and held him. "I know you say you'll protect me, and I'm grateful for that, believe me, but you don't know how cruel he can be. I have to make sure I can look after myself too, in case you're not with me every minute of the day or night."

Jim gave me a kiss on the forehead. "Okay, I understand. It's good. I'm glad to see you've taken a stand and you're not letting that maniac get to you."

I got my fanny pack out of the bedroom closet and took out the bear spray. If Robert came for me, he wouldn't find the old Andrea, meek, trying to please, and easy to bully. I was going to turn a corner right now. No more shaking and worrying and cowering. "If that bastard comes for me, he'll regret it."

"That he will. If I get my hands on him, I'll kill the fucker."

I threw the orchids in the garbage. I'd always loved orchids. Robert had ruined that for me. Bastard! What a weirdo to be so hung up about bloody orchids. Well, there was no way I was having orchids in my house ever again.

Over the next weeks, Jim went shopping with me. Practically everywhere I went, he came with me, never letting me out of his sight. I don't think he believed me about Robert being around. But regardless, he did his best to build up my confidence and get me back to normal. He was thoughtful. Brought me flowers—not orchids—every week.

We had the wildest sex. I hadn't dreamed it could be like that. After that one quick missionary-style coupling last summer, just barely out of sight of the dirt road outside of Masset, I expected sex with Jim to be conservative thereafter. I couldn't have been more wrong. I was physically and mentally fragile then, and Jim knew it. Had to give him credit for taking my feelings into consideration back then. But now? He was a tiger in bed or maybe a stallion ... or a.... Anyway, the sex was incredible and he wanted it all the time. So had Robert, but with him it was more like his weapon. Jim was gentle and loving. I knew it from that one time we made love last summer between fishing trips in Masset. Until then, I had almost forgotten how sex was supposed to be—two people showing their love and passion for each other. I was so shocked to be reminded of how it could—and should be. I had sobbed into his shoulder that time.

He must have wondered what he'd done wrong, but the truth was he'd done everything right. With Jim, it was making love. With Robert, I was just being fucked. Jim showed me that it could be a beautiful thing. I could take more of that beautiful thing any time he wanted.

One time we were in the middle of cooking together. He poured us a glass of red wine and turned up the Pavarotti CD he had playing.

"Won't your neighbours complain?" I asked.

"What neighbours? They're all at least a hundred metres away, and all the trees muffle the sound." He pulled me close for a hug and a long kiss. "Mmm ... lips of wine," he said.

"Yours too," I mumbled as he kissed me again. His lips were soft and warm and yet his cheeks were lean and hard on mine. The beginnings of stubble waiting for the next shave felt raspy on the top of my lips. Not comfortable, but I loved that manliness. "Is it hot in here, or is it me?"

"Well, we are in the kitchen, and it is rather warm," he said. "I think we're overdressed. And yes, you're right. I'm kind of hot too."

"But what about the spaghetti on the stove?"

He smirked. "I'm sure it's pretty hot too, but we can turn it down for a few minutes."

"We'll have to hurry so it doesn't boil over."

"Me too," he said. "No time for the bedroom." He grabbed my hand and tugged me towards the kitchen table.

Chapter 10

Just about ready to go?" I called out. My fingers tapped out a rhythm on the stair railing. I couldn't wait to see Andrea's face when she saw the surprise I had in store for her.

"Almost," she said. "Be right there."

She'd been so upset about the orchids. Seemed like a small thing to get so emotional about, but I knew she'd been through a lot. She was sure Robert had put them there. I insisted that Giselle or one of her friends had done it. They had the keys to my place because they always looked after it when I was away fishing, so they probably wanted to make Andrea feel welcome and bought them to surprise her. Well, they sure did surprise her, but not in a good way. She was so on about this Robert obsession that I decided to give her a little surprise myself and try to make her forget Robert.

Andrea came out of the bedroom. She looked smashing in lavender—the blouse was exactly the colour of her eyes. God, I loved that girl. She wore the flip-flops Giselle had thrown into the clothes bag she'd brought over that first day, but she'd need proper shoes soon. Summer was ending and her ankle was almost back to normal. She was mending fast.

"We need to get you a pair of shoes soon. Maybe today?" We would get shoes, but today I had something else in mind. She leaned forward and kissed my cheek. "Thanks, Jim," she said softly, "for everything."

I just have a short stop to make before we go for groceries and shoes." I glanced over at her and let my hand rest on her thigh.

She laid her hand on mine and patted it gently. "Of course. We can do whatever you want. I have nowhere else I need to be—or want to be, for that matter."

I liked that about her—that she was so obliging and not just thinking about herself all the time. So unlike Sarah who had wanted me all to herself but on her terms.

I turned my old truck into the Toyota parking lot. "Come in with me. There's something I want you to see."

Her brow wrinkled. "Okay.... Are you kicking tires today?"

"Something like that."

The salesman saw me coming and hurried over. "It'll be brought around in just a minute." He spoke into his cell phone and then put it in his pocket.

I introduced Andrea and he shook her hand just a little bit too long. He had a hard time keeping his gaze on her face.

"Erm...." I cleared my throat and he quickly dropped her hand. "We have some paperwork to finish up?"

"Right this way." We followed him to a corner desk where a young woman with a briefcase waited. More introductions followed.

Andrea looked confused. Through the floor-to-ceiling plate glass windows I saw the blue Camry pull up outside. "Excuse us a moment, please. We'll be right back." I steered Andrea towards the door and out to the waiting car. The attendant gave me the keys and left us standing by the open car door.

She grabbed my arm and gave me a puzzled look. "What's going on, Jim?"

"Get in and try it out for size? I need to know if it's comfortable."

Andrea got into the car. I could see her relax into the seat back and close her eyes. "Yes, it's comfortable. Why? Are you thinking of trading in your truck?"

"Oh!" I laughed. "I could never trade in my truck."

"Well, then why am I sitting in this ... what is it? A Camry?"

"I just needed to know if you like it, because the papers are all ready to sign. I'm buying it for you."

Andrea's mouth fell open and her eyes widened. "What?! No way! You're not!" She was beaming a huge smile my way. I'm sure my expression mirrored hers. I leaned into the car and gave her a kiss. Tears filled her eyes.

I pulled away. "What's wrong? You don't like it? Is it the colour? We can change it."

"No, no. It's beautiful." She reached for me and pressed her soft lips on mine. "I just can't believe it. But this is too much. Jim you can't mean it. This is so generous and thoughtful of you."

"I love you, Andrea. Nothing is too good for you. We just have to get the insurance and then you can take it for a spin."

"Thank you," she whispered. "Thank you so much." She held her cheeks with the palms of her hands. "Oh my God, I still can't believe it!" She let out a whoop. Her eyes were filled with tears, happy ones, I presumed.

Chapter 11

I thought I'd hurry and go check the boat while Andrea was out getting groceries. I was looking forward to making a steak dinner for her on the barbecue. She'd do the pasta and veggies and I'd do the rest. I'd buy a couple of nice tenderloin steaks and a bottle of Black Swan shiraz on the way home from the wharf.

Things had been going along really well, at least as far as I could tell, except for an argument we'd had last week. Sometime when the situation wasn't as touchy we would have to revisit that one. But for the most part, Andrea seemed to be enjoying her independence to come and go as she pleased with the Camry. At first I went everywhere with her mainly to give her confidence and to show her that Robert's appearances were all in her head—not that she'd ever admit it. I never pressed the point though. Just hoped she would get over it in time.

We had both been looking forward to tonight's supper. Andrea told me she was thrilled that we'd be eating beef instead of venison for a change. When she was with Robert that's the only red meat they ate, she said. Makes sense if you live way out in the middle of nowhere without a store nearby. Without any kind of house nearby, for that matter. What a way to live. He must have liked that. Total control over her. No one around to keep him in check. He always was a bit of a control freak.

It was only later, when she was getting into the car and I asked her how she liked the new Camry, she acted funny and I realized that I must have struck a nerve. Hadn't realized that she had given up a lot of her independence to live with me. But whatever was bothering her, we could talk about it tonight and fix it.

Since I was going to get the steaks and wine on my way home, I looked for my better jeans. The ratty ones were okay for working on the boat but I wanted to look decent in town and for Andrea when she came home.

I flipped through my closet. Where the hell were all my jeans?

A horrible thought went through my mind as I replayed a scene from only a few days ago.

Not seeing my jeans thrown over the chair where I left them, I had gone to the closet to look for another pair. A whole section was empty.

I scratched my head. "Andrea, can you come here for a sec?"

She hurried over to the bedroom closet. "Yeah? What is it?"

I stretched out my arm and waved it back and forth in the empty space where my pants should have been. "My pants? Where are they?"

She shrugged her shoulders. "I don't know. Did you put them someplace else?"

"No," I said, maybe with a little more sarcasm than I intended. "Did you?"

She straightened up and put her shoulders back. "Of course not! Why would I have moved your jeans?"

"Well, okay." I gave my head a shake. "Let me start over." I took a deep breath. "Did you maybe decide all my pants needed washing?"

"For God's sake, Jim. I've got enough to do without looking for more jobs." She stared at me as if she couldn't believe what I was saying. "Are you serious? Where are all your pants?"

"Jesus, Andrea. There are only two people living in this house. And no pets. We can't even say, 'The dog did it.' Now what did you do with my pants?" I was getting louder, but it was too late, I was so pissed off.

Andrea's voice became shaky. "Jim, I don't know what you're doing, but you're scaring me. I don't know anything about your pants and you're starting to sound like Robert."

"Fuck Robert! Don't you dare compare me to him. It's you trying to fuck with my head."

Andrea's face twisted and she burst into tears. "You men are all the same," she shouted. I could hear her sobbing as she hurried out of the room.

I let out a big sigh and sat on the edge of the bed where we had so recently made love. "That went well." I grabbed my head in my hands. "Oh, crap. I still have to find my pants."

I walked quietly down the hall, trying not to look at where Andrea sat crying in the living room. I opened the laundry chute door and stuck my head in to see ... a huge pile of pants at the bottom.

"So you did put them down the laundry chute."

"Are they there?" she asked in a stuffed up voice.

"You know they are." I went downstairs and brought them all back to the closet. I heaped them on the bed, pulled out a pair and got the hell out of there to go check on the boat.

She must have some awful things going on in her head after all that trauma with Robert. I didn't want to push it, but still.... So this dinner was going to be my way of making it up to her for not understanding. Had to tread carefully though. She still wouldn't admit to doing it.

So here I was again, no pants in the closet. I went straight to the laundry chute. Yup! There they were. I ran my hands through my hair. *Sonofabitch!* This was getting to be a bit much.

I grabbed the bundle of pants and brought them upstairs. I didn't have time to hang them all up again. Dammit! Andrea could hang them up. It's the least she could do after her sick joke. We would have to have a serious talk about this. Tonight's dinner plans were now on shaky ground.

Still, I would do what I said I was going to do—pick up the steaks and wine. At least one of us had to be reliable. I really hadn't thought Andrea was capable of acting out like that. Kind of like a disturbed person. I was starting to have niggling doubts about her. Maybe I had rushed into this relationship too quickly.

I stuffed my wallet in my back pocket and my keys in the front and away I went. Two steps later, my keys slithered down my leg and fell out on the floor. Must have a hole in the pocket. I reached in and my hand went right through to my thighs. I felt for my wallet. It was sliding down towards the back of my leg too. What the hell? Off with the pants. I turned them inside out. All four pockets had been cut open. I picked up another pair of pants. Checked the pockets. Same thing. I scrabbled through all the pants on the chair and every one had the pockets cut out. That bitch! This was not funny anymore. No bloody way I was cooking a lovey-dovey make up dinner tonight.

Chapter 12

"Hey, Jim! Nice to see you. Come in, come in. How are you?" Giselle reached out to kiss me on each cheek, French style. "Cup of coffee for you? Jacques and I were just going to have some."

I stepped inside and put my cap on her end table in the hall. "Have you ever known a fisherman to say no to a cup of coffee?"

"What brings you here today?" Giselle shouted over the electric coffee grinder.

"Just wanted to chat." I nodded to Jacques and shook his hand as he came into the living room.

Giselle brought a plate of homemade chocolate chip cookies into the living room and we each grabbed one.

"I wahdded to...." I waved my hands, signalling that I shouldn't have talked with my mouth crammed full of cookies. "I wanted to ask you again about that day when you took Andrea shopping. I know it's a few weeks ago now, but the orchid issue is still unresolved. And there have been some other odd things going on...."

"The first day? When she first arrived?" She poured the coffee. "That was some funny shopping day."

"Why funny?"

"Well, I don't know if I should tell you all this. I don't want to make trouble for Andrea...." Giselle winced and busied herself with the cream and sugar.

"Go on, Giselle," Jacques said. "You need to tell Jim, so he can deal with it."

Giselle hesitated and then shrugged. "I suppose you need to know. When you phoned me I tried to make it sound not so bad, but then I got thinking about it and ... well ... just be careful how you talk to her about it."

"Okay," I said. "I can do that. So what happened?"

"She was really, really freaked out about that guy she was living with. She told me he tried to talk to her as she was getting in the car. That was after the hairdresser's. I looked over. There was nobody by the car. Andrea was screaming at me to 'Go, go, go!' Even with the doors locked she was so scared. She was shaking and crying. I felt sorry for her. But nobody was there."

"You went shopping after that?"

"She wanted to go home but I knew you wanted her to get some clothes, so I convinced her to come into Courtenay to some shops. I thought everything was okay."

"And it wasn't?"

"We were riding along through town and she turned white and shaky. She said she'd seen him again."

"Did she?"

"I don't think so. I think she's so freaked out by this guy she's seeing him everywhere. What the hell did he do to her anyway?"

I let out a big sigh. "Oh, I think it was a nightmare for her. Not just the beatings, but the mental abuse. He had her so scared. When he didn't hit her she was always afraid he would. And he was always telling her how stupid she was."

"She told you this?" Giselle shook her head. "My God, it's hard to believe a man could do this."

"Believe me, Robert is capable of all of that. I've seen him in action a few times. He has a mean streak in him. But then he's all apologetic afterwards."

"Typical abuser." Jacques spoke only for the second time. I had almost forgotten he was there.

"So one thing I really need to know.... See, when we got home from the movie that night, we sat in the living room with a glass of brandy. I told her I liked the flowers, and she nearly went off the deep end."

"What flowers?" Giselle asked.

I stopped breathing for a moment while an image of Robert with orchids flashed through my head. "I was afraid you'd say that. So you didn't bring them?"

Giselle shook her head. "What kind of flowers?"

"Orchids. Robert's favourite. The kind he used to give her."

"I can see that," she said. "Very expensive. Makes a statement."

"These were in a little pot...." I studied Giselle's face, looking for a smile to crack and for her to burst out laughing to say it was all a bad joke, but her expression was poker straight. "You didn't put them there? Maybe just playing a joke on us?"

"No, I swear I didn't, Jim. Flowers would have been nice, but I didn't think of it.... Maybe just as well, if it upset her so much."

"It wasn't the flowers. It was the fact that they were orchids."

"So what do you think?" Jacques asked. "Do you think it was Robert? In your house? *Merde!*"

"I've been trying to believe it's all in Andrea's head, but *somebody* had to put those flowers there. I haven't mentioned it to her, hoping she'd forgotten about them, but I haven't been able to figure out how they got in the house."

"For sure it wasn't us."

I got up to leave, thanking them for the goodies.

"You be careful, Jim. I don't like the sound of this." Giselle took Jacques by the arm. "That's a little bit scary."

A creepy feeling spread over my skin and I shivered involuntarily. *He was in my house! That's why the porch light was off. That's who cut the pants pockets. That's who threw the pants down the laundry chute.*

Chapter 13

The Camry was a beauty. Every time I looked at it, I was reminded that Jim loved me. *I know he loves me.* Sure we'd had some ups and downs lately. We worked through that little episode about the jeans being in the laundry. Weird that he got so upset when he forgot that he'd put them all down the chute. I still didn't understand what that was all about—how he could forget something like that.

I was about to get into the car to go grocery shopping. Beautiful as it was, I still didn't feel right about him buying it for me. Jim came out and asked if I wanted him to do steaks on the barbecue. "Wow! Yeah! What's not to like about that offer?"

"So what do you think about the car now that you've had a chance to drive it a few times?"

I nodded. "It's good."

"And?"

"And what?" I wasn't sure what he wanted me to say.

Jim had furrows in his brow. "That's all? Just good?"

I raised my hands, palms upward to say, *What do you want from me?* "Yes, and of course, I love it...."

"But...."

I blew out the breath I'd been holding. "But you shouldn't have bought it for me."

Jim took a step closer to me and studied my face. "What do you mean?"

I shrugged, squirming inside. Whatever I said now was going to hurt his feelings. Too late to backtrack. "It's such a big gift."

Jim gave his shoulders a quick shrug. "Not a big deal."

"It is to me."

"I don't see what the problem is."

"Look, Jim. It's really sweet that you bought me the car. It's kind of you to pay for my clothes. You pay for my food. I live in your house. You buy my shoes, for God's sake." I felt my voice rising as my emotions threatened to spill over.

"What's wrong with that? You do things for me."

"Like what?"

"You cook for us. You keep the house and garden nice. And we have great sex together."

"So that makes me a maid, a cook, a gardener, and a prostitute."

"Aw, Andrea. Don't do this. Everything has been so good."

"Yeah, for you—" As soon as the words were out of my mouth I felt ungrateful. I didn't know what was wrong with me, pouring out all these penned up feelings.

Jim's eyebrows went up and he pointed at his chest. "For me? I'm the one who's paying."

My throat tightened into a knot. "I never asked you to."

He reached over and took me by the arm. "I know, I know. But I wanted you to have everything, be happy...."

I took Jim's hand off my arm. "I know, and it was good for me that you helped me when I was down, but...."

He stood there, arms dangling limply. "But what?"

I knew I'd been really lucky to be in Jim's life. And then it hit me. That's what the problem was. Jim wasn't in my life. I was in his. What had happened to *my* life?

"I feel so useless, worthless. No personal goals, no pride. I've lost who I once was. I'm not me anymore."

Jim looked stunned. He didn't say a word.

"I think I need to look for a job." I got into the car, backed it out and drove up the long driveway. When I looked in the rear view mirror, my stomach clenched and tears welled in my eyes to see Jim standing there with his shoulders slumped and a dejected look on his face.

I left my resumé at the two insurance companies in town and at a print shop where I would take passport photos. I even applied for a job as a wharfinger's helper. I had a lot of experience from when I had that job in Lund and met Robert, that mental nutcase who nearly ruined my life. I met Jim there too, and that's what I would remember. If I got this job, I would be able to see Jim whenever he was down at the wharf checking his boat.

I felt better applying for those jobs, even if I hadn't been hired yet. It would be good to have a bit of money of my own again. It had been too long. The whole time I was with Robert, I had no bank account, no car, no phone, no job, no friends, no independence, and no hope. That would change now.

Next, I opened a bank account in town and deposited $25 of Jim's money. I'd pay him back. I owed him a lot for all he'd done for me. Taking some steps in the right direction was encouraging.

I bought some fancy salad in a bag to have with our steak dinner and promised myself I'd talk things through with Jim and get him to understand that I needed to be me again.

Chapter 14

I had the steaks marinating in garlic and olive oil. The Shiraz was cool, not cold, just right. Two glasses stood ready, but Andrea still wasn't home from grocery shopping. I looked at the clock. She should have been home by now.

To hell with it. I'll have a glass of wine while I wait for her. I'd have to admit I was out of line about the pants. I know it had to have been Robert. A shudder ran over my shoulders. When did he do it? How did he get in?

Jesus, what if he had a key? He would be able to let himself in here any time he wanted. Holy shit! He could be in the house right now. I searched the place and then called the first locksmith I found in the yellow pages. Told him I'd pay extra but he had to come over and change those locks right now.

Dinner would be late. That was all right. Andrea wasn't home yet anyway.

Five o'clock. So where was she? I should have insisted she get a cell phone. Stupid of me not to take care of that.

She'd said something about looking for a pair of shoes before she got the groceries, so maybe that took longer than she expected.

I refilled my glass and set it on the coffee table. Somehow I didn't feel like drinking it now without Andrea. God, I'd yelled at her about the pants. I must have sounded just like Robert. And I wasn't very understanding about how buying the car might make her feel. I was so lucky to have her and if I didn't watch it I was going to blow it. She could have any guy she wanted. Best thing that ever happened to me was to find her. I'd had girlfriends before, but never someone so real. Someone so genuine. She never put on false airs, pretending to be something she's not. *What you see is what you get.* My kind of girl.

And that comment about her being my maid and gardener and a prostitute. Shit! I must have been blind not to realize how she felt. No money of her own and really down on her luck, she must have thought she had no options and I was taking advantage of her. Man, I had some serious repair work to do to make it up to her.

The locksmith arrived. He had all the new assemblies ready to go. The pick-proof kind this time. Didn't take him all that long. Six-thirty already. What the hell was keeping Andrea? I phoned Giselle.

"Is Andrea over there with you?"

"No. Isn't she home?" A chill crept over me. "Jim? What's going on?" Giselle sounded worried.

"She's not back from grocery shopping. She was going to get a pair of shoes too, but still, it shouldn't take her this long."

Chapter 15

After three weeks, I was getting a bit tired of the games. I had wanted to make Jim's life hell and maybe he'd get tired of Andrea, kick her out, and I'd be here waiting for her, but this was dragging on too long. He should have kicked her out after the pants episode, but he seemed to have more patience than I would have had. This wasn't working. I needed to get her back. Now.

I sat in my truck by one of the group mailboxes that overlooked the road from Jim's place. Thank God I was a reader and could entertain myself. Reading had always been a good escape when times were bad. And they were bad a lot. I took out my book while I watched for Andrea's blue Camry. It wasn't all that long before she drove by.

I gave her lots of space and then pulled in behind her.

I waited while she went into two insurance offices, the wharfinger's office, and a print shop. Followed her to Superstore and waited while she did her shopping. She came out with a couple of bags in her cart.

I got out and walked towards her while she put the bags in the trunk. Just then a car pulled into the parking space on the other side of her and a big bruiser of a woman got out. She stood at the back of her car, right beside Andrea.

"I'll give you a loonie for the cart, so you don't have to take it back," she said. Andrea nodded sure, and the woman fished around in her purse while Andrea closed the trunk and unlocked her car door. I couldn't do anything with the big woman standing right there and I couldn't stand there gawking at the two of them. I turned around quickly so Andrea wouldn't see me. As soon as the woman left with her cart, I rushed up to Andrea's car door. She was already in and when she saw me, she slammed the button down to lock it, panic written all over her face. I couldn't let her leave now. I banged on the window. Hard.

"Andrea, wait!" Then I calmed myself down, doing a quick count to ten. I took a deep breath and said in a normal voice, "Please, I just want to talk to you." I gave her my sweetest, most desperate smile.

She opened the window about half an inch. "Leave me alone," she shouted.

"I just want to talk. I won't hurt you. Please, Andrea. Look, you don't want me hanging around all the time, so will you come have a cup of coffee with me and we'll talk it through and get things settled.

"Are you kidding me? Go to hell!" She started the car.

"Wait, Andrea." I talked fast, so she wouldn't leave. "Just hear me out. Ricky's Restaurant is right over there. Lots of people around so you don't have to worry. Nothing's going to happen to you. You want this to stop, don't you?" I could see her starting to cave, so I added a little, "Please?"

But then she shook her head. "I don't trust you. Why would I go have a coffee with you?"

I took another deep breath, unclenched my jaw, and tried once more, remembering to sound calm and gentle. "We need to get this settled once and for all. You don't want me hanging around and following you all the time, do you?"

"How do I know you won't hurt me?"

Now to drive the last nail home. "There are lots of people in Ricky's. You'd be really safe and we could talk things through and get back to a normal life. You'd like that, wouldn't you?"

"If I do, will you go back to Powell River and leave me alone?"

"I promise I won't hurt you and I'll leave you alone." Had her! "C'mon, let me buy you a coffee." *And you can make my coffee forever after like a good wife should.*

She turned off the engine and got out of the car. She stumbled on her sore ankle and I reached out to catch her, but she jumped back as if I'd burned her.

"Okay, okay," I said, throwing my arms up in a hands-off gesture. "Just trying to help."

Andrea held up her palms ready to push me away. "Don't touch me or even get close to me." She started to walk towards the Ricky's Restaurant. "I shouldn't even be doing this, but if it will make you stop...."

Chapter 16

I stuck my hands in my pockets to hide the fact that they were shaking again. I should have my head examined. Here I was going into a restaurant with Robert, who terrified me. What was the matter with me? But I had to make this nightmare stop. If I could get him to promise to stay away, make him realize it was hopeless, maybe he would leave Jim and me alone. I glanced up at Robert's face. Couldn't believe I ever thought he was handsome. All I saw now was ugliness. His eyes were narrowed and his jaw set. It had always been hard to read his emotions. He had that intense look even when he was relaxed—as relaxed as Robert ever got. It frightened me to be so close to him again, but I had made a vow to myself to be tougher and if this was going to end the stalking then it was worth suffering for a little while. Jim would be so glad that it would all be over and we could be a normal couple with Robert out of the picture.

Ricky's was right beside Superstore, so there were lots of people around and all I had to do was yell, and the police station was just across the street. I didn't think of it as a stupid move, but rather as the new me, facing problems head on instead of being a wimp and feeling so victimized. I had promised myself I wasn't going to be weak anymore and this would be a step in the right direction ... I hoped.

Robert opened the door for me and we found a booth by the window. He couldn't hurt me here.

"You're looking great, Andrea," Robert said. "Beautiful," he whispered under his breath.

"Look, Robert. Don't get the wrong idea. Just because I came here with you." I sat up straight as the waitress came over to take our order. "Peppermint tea, please." I wasn't ordering anything that would take long to serve or eat. I wasn't staying long.

"Cup of coffee and a doughnut please."

"I'm sorry, we don't have doughnuts. Apple turnover?"

Robert's face clouded over. "Fine." I could sense the tightness in his voice. He still had the potential to blow up. I would have to be careful.

When the waitress left I kept my voice low. "So why are you following me around, Robert? Can't you see it's over?"

"It'll never be over, Andrea. You're my wife. I want you to come home."

"That's not going to happen. You've hit me too many times. You're never going to hit me again."

He nodded. "That's exactly what I was going to tell you. I'm never going to hit you again. So it's okay for you to come home."

I leaned away in disbelief, throwing my back into the booth wall. "You're unbelievable." I laughed. "Literally.... I can't believe a word you say. Do you know how many times you've said that? 'I'm never going to hit you again.' You can't really think I'd believe you."

He sat up taller and stuck his chin out. "Of course you can believe me!"

I shook my head. "I was hoping you would say you'd leave me alone after this."

He reached for my hand and I snapped it off the table. "Andrea, I love you. Can't you see that? I can't live without you." His face took on a hurt expression, like he really believed what he was saying. What a master he was at putting on a most angelic facial expression.

I rolled my eyes. "Oh, come on!"

Our tea and coffee arrived and we stopped talking for a moment. Once the waitress had left, I said, "You promised that if I came here with you, you were going to stop bothering me." My hand shook as I reached for my tea. Dammit. I didn't want him to see me cowering and trembling. I picked up the cup in two hands and had a sip. "So why don't you go back to Lund or Powell River or wherever you have the boat now and just forget about me."

"I can't do that, Andrea." His eyes changed from the hurt look and seemed to glaze over and stare as if they were burning holes into me. Such glaring, penetrating eyes. I shuddered involuntarily and fought the urge to throw up from fear. I had forgotten how he always stared so intensely. It terrified me so much I had to make a conscious effort not to pee my pants. I had to fight to hold my body together and not let it betray me.

"Cold?" he asked.

I put my shoulders back. "Must be the air-conditioning blowing on me." No way I wanted to appear weak. "I was hoping you'd say we should get a divorce and you'd agree not to come around. You could live your life. Jim and I could live ours."

"Jim! Hah!" he snorted. "My best friend runs off with my wife and I'm supposed to sit back and take it? My *best* friend!"

"Sh-h-h! Keep your voice down."

"My *best* friend!" he repeated.

Your only friend. "Well, you can see how bad it was then, if even your best friend won't support wife beating." I pushed my cup towards the middle of the table and slid out of the booth. "We're done here."

Robert was fast. His hand snapped an iron grip onto my wrist and bent it towards me so I had to sit down again.

He must have assumed I wouldn't want to make a scene because he looked surprised when I said, "If you don't let go this second, I'm going to yell for the police."

He let go instantly. I got up again. "I'm going now. I was foolish to think you would be reasonable."

Robert's voice was low and threatening. "You leave now, I'll find you. I promised to be nice to you. But you're my wife. It's your duty to come with me." He stood at the end of the booth now, towering over me. I made a move to push past him and head towards the door, but he grabbed my wrist again and walked with me. His hand was like a pair of vise grips.

The hostess at the till by the door looked our way. "Call 9-1-1," I shouted to her.

"No! It's okay." Robert motioned for her relax. "It's okay. She's my wife."

"Call 9-1-1," I repeated, louder. "I'm not going with him. Call now, please."

Robert clamped a hand over my mouth, twisted my arm behind my back and propelled me out the door as the hostess punched numbers into the phone. A couple of customers came running out after us, yelling for Robert to stop, but he took long strides towards a mint green truck. He opened the canopy at the back, lifted me up, and threw me in as if I were a sack of potatoes. I'd forgotten how strong he was. I tumbled into the back of the truck scraping my hands in an effort to break my fall, hitting my head on the inside of the window frame. I tried to turn the handle of the canopy door, yelling as loud as I could. It was too late. I heard the key turn in the lock.

Robert peeled out of the parking lot as if the place was on fire. I peeked through the tiny canopy window as he sped up the hill away from town. I prayed for a police car to be following us, but no such luck.

Oh Jim, I'm so sorry. I've gone and made a stupid move again. I hugged myself, trembling and sobbing. *Come find me, Jim. Save me from this crazy monster. Please, hurry!*

Chapter 17

I couldn't stand it anymore. I jumped into the truck and drove to Superstore where Andrea said she was going to do the shopping. The parking lot was only about a third full. I spotted her Camry right away. I looked inside. Nothing unusual. I went into the store and raced up and down the aisles. Then I thought, why waste time, I could have her paged. I tapped my foot and drummed my fingers on the service counter while they called her name over the PA system. It was a big store so I should allow time for her to get to the customer service area, but I had a feeling she wouldn't be coming. After five precious minutes of wasted time, I left the store.

Back out at the car, I tried my key in the trunk. There were two bags of groceries. So she'd done the shopping, but where the hell was she? I felt the milk carton. It wasn't all that cold anymore. I slammed the trunk down and scanned the parking lot. No sign of her.

Shit! This could be bad. My insides knotted up and fear sent a shot of adrenaline through me. I had a pretty good idea what might have happened and the thought made my knees quake. Robert would have had no trouble forcing her into a vehicle. Not only was he a big guy, but he could be very persuasive or threatening, whichever method suited him in getting what he wanted. I'd seen him in action often enough in altercations on the wharf.

Most of the shops in the strip mall next to the Superstore were closed, but maybe she'd gone into Tim

Horton's or Ricky's. I dashed over to Ricky's first. It was the closest. I scanned the restaurant. Not there.

"Are you meeting someone?" the hostess asked.

"No, I was just wondering if my girlfriend was here. Her car's outside and I thought she might have come in here."

The hostess stood up a little straighter and took a deep breath. "What does she look like?"

I fought back tears as I pictured her in my mind. "Dark chestnut hair just past her shoulders, about your height, maybe 5 ft. 4. Mid-twenties. Very pretty. Slight limp from a sprained ankle."

The hostess grabbed my arm. "She was here arguing with a big guy. She wanted to leave by herself but he said she was his wife. Is she married?" She let go of my arm and took a step back. "Maybe I've got the wrong person."

"No, that sounds like her." I looked towards the door. "Where is she?"

"She yelled for me to dial 9-1-1. He took her outside and put her in a truck—in the back—just picked her up and threw her in." The wide-eyed hostess shook her head. "Then he locked the canopy door. Some people watched but they were all afraid to do anything. He was a big guy."

"Damn him!" I clenched my fists, yet felt so helpless. My worst fears were coming true.

The hostess shrugged. "I did call the police and they came right away."

I perked up. "How long ago was that?"

"About half an hour?"

I dashed past her, calling thanks over my shoulder. I couldn't get to the police station fast enough.

It was just across the street. I screeched to a stop in the RCMP parking lot and rushed for the door. Locked! "Ring the buzzer," a sign said. I pushed the button repeatedly until someone came on the intercom. I told them I had some information on the abduction case they'd just been called out on. Hurry! It was urgent.

The officer on duty led me into an interview room and a Constable John Creston came to talk to me almost instantly. I gave him my name and address.

"My girlfriend, Andrea, is missing. Her car's just over there in the Superstore lot." I waved in the general direction of the store. "Her husband tried to kill her not so long ago. He's been stalking her. I'm sure he's taken her."

"We did have an incident at Ricky's. Can you give us a description of Andrea?"

I rattled off the description as fast as I could. No time to waste. "27 years old, 5-4, dark brown hair just past her shoulders. Violet eyes. Pretty."

"And Robert?"

"Tall, maybe 6-3, muscular. Good looking. Dark hair, hawkish nose. Big guy. Mentally unstable."

"Any idea where he might take her?"

"Powell River," I blurted out. "He has his troller there, or Lund." Now that I said it out loud, I knew just where he would be. "He'll most likely try to get on the next ferry. I've got to go get her."

"Here's my card. Don't do anything foolish. I'll make some calls and get a patrol car out there to the ferry."

Chapter 18

I couldn't take Andrea straight to the ferry like I wanted to and have them find her in the back of the truck when I bought my ticket.

I hadn't expected her to actually go to Ricky's with me. Now that I had her, I needed a plan. And fast. I had the date rape drugs stashed in the glove compartment, had them for weeks, for whenever I might be able to grab her. They would come in handy today.

I drove along a by-road beside the beach in the area past the ferry terminal and found a place to pull off. I unlocked the canopy and lifted the door. She scurried to the back without having to be told. Her eyes were huge with fear. Good! That was best for the time being. I crawled in and pulled the canopy door shut behind me.

She had her back pressed into the far corner of the truck box, looking like a cornered animal. Exactly what she was. All under my control. *That's how it should be. How it should always be.* "Now, Andrea. I need you to co-operate with me. We can do this the hard way or the easy way. Hard way," I showed her my fist up close and made her suck in her breath—I loved it, "I punch you in the face and knock you out, so you look like you're sleeping when we get to the ferry. Easy way, you take one of my sleeping pills which won't hurt you a bit, and you'll sleep through the whole thing. I won't touch you as long as you do as I tell you." She cowered pale-faced in the corner. "So what's it going to be? Hard?" I showed her my fist. She flinched. "Or easy?" I waved the pill bottle in front of her. She nodded.

"Good choice, girl. I'll even let you come sit up front once the pill takes effect." She would be very docile by the time we got in the 7:15 ferry lineup to Powell River. Stupid bimbo, believing it was just a sleeping pill.

Two of you?" the ferry employee asked. "She looks tired."

I glanced over at Andrea. Her head was slumped down, chin on her chest. "Too much wine at supper." I gave the ferry employee a shrug, trying my best to look embarrassed.

The employee smiled and nodded. "Any pets in the back?"

"Nope." *Just my little pet here in the front.* I handed her my Visa. I knew I could be tracked by it, but I wanted her to think this was just another normal day for me. And anyway, so what if anyone challenged me? She was MY wife!

The ticket seller handed my Visa back. "Lane 7, please. Have a nice evening."

"Same to you." Had to work at keeping my jubilation under control. *Yes, yes, yes!* I hissed to myself as I pulled into Lane 7. *Let the fun and games begin.*

Chapter 19

The constable made a call as soon as I told him Robert's name and where I thought he was probably headed. It was good to know they were on their way, in case I didn't get there first.

I hurried out of the police station. The ferry terminal was just up the hill and down again to the left. I was going to get that sonofabitch. Mint green truck with a white canopy, the constable had said. *Shouldn't be hard to spot.*

Now that I thought about it, I had seen a mint green truck in our mailbox area a few times in the past weeks but hadn't thought much about it. So he'd been hanging around, watching, for some time already.

At the ferry terminal I pulled into the foot passenger parking area and jumped out. A quick scan of the ferry lines and Bingo! There it was.

"Be right back," I called over my shoulder to the attendant as I sprinted towards the truck. I was almost there when a dark gray sedan whizzed past me and screeched to a stop three car lengths behind Robert's truck. Two RCMP members jumped out. They waved for me to back off. Hands on their holsters, they approached Robert's truck, one on each side.

"Step out of the truck, Sir," one of the members said. "Keep your hands where I can see them."

I heard Robert say something, questioning them, no doubt, playing the innocent. "Step out of the truck," the cop repeated.

I could hardly restrain myself from running over to yank that bastard out of the truck and take Andrea out of there. I was sure he had her in there. But I had to defer to the officers in their effort to do it the right way. They had told me to stay back and I didn't want to mess up their operation.

Robert opened the truck door and slowly got out. He pulled himself to his full height and looked straight at the cop.

"Turn around. Put your hands on the hood." Robert took his time, but did as he was told. The constable took Robert's knife out of its carrying case on his belt. "Are you carrying any other weapons? Anything sharp in your pockets?"

"Just my knife," he said.

"What do you have a knife for?" the constable asked.

Robert's tone was belligerent. "I'm a fisherman. All fishermen carry a knife."

"Who is your passenger?"

"My wife," he challenged, his chin rising.

The other policeman waved me over. By this time I had crept closer anyway. "Is this Andrea?"

I nodded. "Yes." I almost choked on the word. She lay slumped in the seat, unconscious, her face sporting a bright red patch that would bruise soon. Her lip was split and dried tear tracks ran down her cheeks. I felt as if my heart stopped. "Yes, that's her. Jesus! What's he done to her? You need to call an ambulance."

"Done. They're on their way."

I cradled Andrea's head in my arms. "Andrea. Can you hear me, sweetheart?"

Robert snarled at me, "She's not your sweetheart. She's mine!"

"And I suppose this is how you treat 'your sweetheart'? I can just see all the love."

He was cuffed, but turned toward me just as they were putting him into the police car. "You wife-stealing sonofabitch. I'll get you. This isn't over. You're going to regret messing with me."

I was so pissed off with Robert for what he was doing to Andrea, it didn't matter that he was three inches taller and many pounds heavier. He could easily lay a beating on me, but right now, I felt I'd kill him with my bare hands if I could get at him. "Bring it on, you sicko!" I shouted.

The constable gave Robert's head an extra nudge as he shoved him into the back of the car.

I turned back to Andrea. All my anger changed to concern in a second. "Sweetheart, can you hear me? Andrea? It's me, Jim." I patted her cheek, trying to waken her. "Andrea? Wake up." I choked back tears. She was breathing, but only shallow breaths. I clutched at her hands and rubbed them. "Wake up, Andrea. Please wake up." I looked at the constable. "What did he do to her? What's wrong with her?"

Why wasn't she waking up? He couldn't have hit her hard enough to knock her out for that long. Or maybe he did and the bruises didn't show yet. I heard the sirens in the distance. About bloody time! If they couldn't bring her back to me, I didn't know what I'd do. I'd be lost without her. If she survived, I knew that sonofabitch wouldn't quit until he killed her. Unless I killed him first.

Chapter 20

Déjà vu. It felt like a re-run. Here I was again in a hospital, sitting by Andrea's bed, waiting for her to wake up. I had dozed in the chair for a while until I heard her groan.

She blinked, trying to open her eyes, frowned, and closed them again. She took a deep breath and raised her eyebrows in an effort to open her eyes and try to get her bearings. "Where ...? Wha ... happened?"

Relief flooded through me. *Oh, thank God she's awake.* I leapt up and took her hand. "Andrea, how are you feeling? Do you hurt anywhere? I was so worried about you." I was aware I was squeezing her hand too tightly, but I was so glad to see her awake. I blinked back the tears I felt building behind my eyes.

She propped herself up on her elbows and looked around the room before focusing on me again. "Jim! Oh ... Jim, you're ... here."

I put my arms around her and pulled her to me tightly. She felt small and frail. I had an overwhelming urge and responsibility to protect her. "I'm so glad you're okay." I kissed her forehead. "How are you feeling?"

"Fuzzy. Wha ... happened?"

"Seems you were right after all. Robert was following you and grabbed you at Ricky's Restaurant." Her brow furrowed and she looked puzzled. "Andrea? Does that ring a bell?"

I helped her sit up and adjusted the pillow behind her back. "I 'member bein' in Ricky's with Rober'. Affer 'at iss all a bit fuzzy." She looked around the room. "Feel sick." I handed her the pan from the night table. She turned on her side and retched, poor thing. I grabbed a tissue and helped dab her mouth clean. "Water?" she whispered, eyes brimming with tears.

I brought her a glass of water and held it to her mouth. "Look. Let's not talk about it until you're feeling better."

"Yeah. Good idea." Her eyes were closing already as she laid her head back on the pillow.

I slept in the chair by her bed that night. If Robert was released from custody I wanted to be sure he didn't try again to nab Andrea. Man! What had I let myself in for? All this drama. My life was humming along just fine until Andrea came along. Not her fault, of course, all this trouble with Robert. Guy's a nutcase! And I wanted Andrea every bit as much as he did but for different reasons. I loved her. To him, she was an obsession. He couldn't take no for an answer.

I looked over at her sleeping in the hospital bed. So helpless and vulnerable. She really had no one to go to bat for her except me. Whether I wanted it or not, I was the one who was dragged into this nightmare with her. I could just walk away, find someone else. But then she'd have no one, and worse yet, I would lose the best thing that had ever happened to me. No. I couldn't walk away, no matter how difficult things might become. I loved her too much. If she was in a messy situation, I was in it with her up to my neck. No way I could leave her. No way I ever would.

I felt sick at the recriminations I'd made, accusing her of hiding my jeans, and thinking she had cut the pockets out of them. It was all Robert's doing. His plan to drive us apart had almost worked.

If only she would bounce back from this, I promised myself I'd do better by her.

The next two days, I took care of Andrea at home. She regained most of her memory up to the point where Robert had given her the pills. We sat on the sofa in the living room with a cup of tea and gradually, the story came out.

"He said if I wanted it to end—his stalking—we should go settle things in the restaurant. I didn't want to go but I did want it to end. So I went. I thought I'd be safe with other people around. Later, I tried to leave and he took hold of my arm and dragged me out of the restaurant. People just stood there, watching and doing nothing. I remember looking at them, calling to them to help me, but they looked as terrified as I felt. Robert threw me into the back of his truck. Later he parked someplace and came into the back of the truck with me. He said I could either take the sleeping pill or he could knock me out with his fist. I took the pill. That's all I remember."

"The doctor said they've done some tests and that wasn't a sleeping pill. It was Rohypnol."

"What's that?" she asked.

"It's like Valium only stronger. They call it the date-rape drug because it knocks you out in about 30 minutes and then when you wake up you don't remember anything."

She slapped a hand over her mouth and groaned. "Oh God! I hope he didn't...."

"The doctor said you were not raped."

Her shoulders slumped. "Oh, thank God." She looked up quickly. "Do you know where Robert is now?"

"Don't worry. The police took him away." I looked down at her hands. The fists had relaxed. I took her fingers and played with them. "I'm sorry I doubted you about Robert." I put my arms around her and rubbed her back. "I'll never doubt you again."

She reached up and stroked my cheek. Her eyes were brimming over with tears. "What would I do without you?"

"You don't have to do without me. I'm going to keep you safe from that crazy, disturbed man."

"I hope they keep him in jail."

"I hope so too. At least for a while," I added, but it reminded me that I should go see the police and find out what was happening to Robert.

I lay awake for a long time that night. We were both tired and stressed out from the Robert situation. In the morning, I ran the idea by Andrea.

"I've been thinking, and I have an idea."

"Yeah?" She waited for me to go on, making impatient rolling motions with her hands.

"I think it would be good for us to get away from all this Robert trouble. Why don't we close up the house and go to Hawaii for a while?"

"Really!?" Her eyes were wide and so was her smile. "You mean it?"

"Of course. We won't have to think about him and we can try to get our lives back to some kind of normal." I smiled to think she was eager for the holiday.

"I've never been to Hawaii," she said, "and I sure would love to be there just with you."

"Great! I figure we have two choices. We can go for two weeks and stay in a condo or some such accommodation. Or we can go for much longer, say two or three months ... or more, and camp instead."

"Camping and long term! No contest," she said.

"Wonderful. I'll start making plans." It would be so good to get away from that leech. I was tired of having him suck the life out of us.

Chapter 21

I lay down on the rock hard bunk and pulled the rough gray blanket over myself. My head was pounding. The jail was noisy even though it was only in the police station. I'd seen movies about prisons and knew if I ever landed there, the noise would push me over the edge of sanity. I had asked for a couple of painkillers but the fuckers just laughed. The only thing that helped my migraines was quiet and darkness. No chance I'd find that here. I'd ram my fist into the wall except it would hurt my head. I wanted to yell obscenities at the cops for putting me here, but it hurt to make any noise louder than a whisper.

The injustice of it all made everything harder to bear. She was MY wife. Why couldn't they see that I had a right to my own wife? I wanted to cry like a baby but I didn't dare. When things went wrong and life was unfair, I had a hard time dealing with it. Always had.

My mother! Hah! She doesn't deserve to be called a mother. She was the epitome of unfairness. My brother Tony and I got more beatings than we would ever want to remember. She must have been pissed off because she didn't have a man. Most women would cry and get depressed. Not her. She'd get mad, and drink, and get madder, and drink more. Then, just before she passed out, look out! If you were in reach, you became her punching bag, and she was no small woman. One time she walloped Tony so hard his head spun around and he lost his balance. He fell backwards hitting his head on the edge of the counter. She kicked at him but then quit. He didn't move. Guess he'd passed out, and that took the fun out of hitting him. I hid in the bedroom until she passed out too, and then I went back to look after Tony. He was still lying there, not moving. I called 9-1-1, and that was it for us living in that house. Tony was never the same after that, but then, neither was I.

Foster care was no fun, but I learned to read to escape, and if kids teased me, I kicked the shit out of them and they never did it again. Talking big saved me a lot of trouble. Hitting put the icing on the cake, as they say. I was good at both. I learned to talk my way into and out of anything I wanted.

If only I didn't get these stress headaches. They hurt like hell.

After a while, a constable unlocked the cell door and snapped handcuffs on me while he led me to a brightly lit room down the hall. The pain from the stabbing light was excruciating. I sat with my head propped in my hands, eyeballs throbbing behind closed lids.

The uniform who came in to talk to me slapped a file folder on the table. The sound reverberated in my brain. The chair scraping the floor set my teeth on edge. I groaned.

"Not feeling well, Mr. Bolton?"

I didn't look up. Didn't open my eyes. "No," I moaned. "Migraine."

"Aw ... that's a crying shame." The sarcasm was just dripping off his tongue. "I'm betting Andrea has a bit of a headache too right now." The cop had no sympathy at all. "Where'd you get the date-rape drug?"

I didn't answer. Just pressed the heels of my hands into my eyeballs.

He slammed his hand on the table. I hated that he made me jump. So humiliating. Just like my bitch of a mother used to do. A jab of pain stabbed my temples. "Answer me," he shouted. The throbbing arrowed from my eyes to my temples and deep into my brain behind my eyes.

"What date-rape drug?" I mumbled.

"We've got you on administering a drug against Andrea's will."

"Oh no, you don't." My voice was dull and probably not convincing, but the pain kept me from stating my case more effectively. I wanted to leap up and punch his lights out, but even that thought hurt my head. "She was looking for something in her purse. Must have been some kind of pill to get high or something. I had nothing to do with that. If she overdosed, it was her own fault. She took it willingly."

"Why would she willingly take a date-rape drug?"

I turned my head to look at the cop and immediately regretted the movement. Felt like my whole brain was bruised and the turn of my head sent another spear of pain through me. "Maybe she didn't know that's what it was. Maybe she thought she was buying something else."

"Well, either way, we've got you for kidnapping."

"I was picking her up after she did our shopping. She's my wife. What the hell else do you want? My wife! She belongs to me." I poked my chest with my finger again and again to make my point. Oh, Christ, my pulse was hammering my eyeballs. "Do I need a lawyer?"

"That's up to you, Mr. Bolton. Do you feel you need one?"

"If you're charging me with something, yes."

He sighed, shook his head, and unlocked my handcuffs. "We're going to release you pending further investigation. You need to get in your truck and go to Powell River. Don't leave the province. Stick close to home. We'll be wanting to talk to you again."

"Told you, you've got nothing."

"Get the fuck outta here, asshole."

Chapter 22

On the ferry ride back to Powell River, I lay down on the old mattress in the back of the truck. The ordeal at the police station had my mind spiralling down into a dark place. I hated everyone—Jim the wife stealer, Andrea the unfaithful bitch, and the cops who were working against me. I was completely justified in what I was doing, so the establishment should have been on my side. The stress and injustice of it got my head pounding like a sledge hammer on steel. The ringing and echoing sent jabs of pain through my skull. It was over an hour before the headache finally began to fade and I felt like going out on deck to sit on a bench. The fresh air helped clear my head and I had time to think.

The Hawkeye was tied to the dock at Finn Bay, just around the corner from Lund. Finn Bay was perfect. It was out of sight and the wharf was small. Only a few boats were there at one time—fewer people to ask a lot of questions. A boatyard was tucked away out of sight at the top of the hill behind the wharf. Just a little gravel parking lot in the bush. I could have the Hawkeye hauled out there so I could work on it without a lot of people noticing the changes I planned to make.

First though, on my way through Powell River, I'd stop at the marine supply store to pick up some gray paint, sandpaper, brushes, rollers, and paint thinner. The bright orange of the Hawkeye would have to go. She would blend in with the sea better if she were a dull colour. I wanted to be as inconspicuous as possible.

Then I'd get rid of those bow poles. I could manage fine without them. It wouldn't be that big of a deal to take them off, and anyway, it would look better. I always thought those two smaller poles looked like a grasshopper's antennae. I could fish just fine without them. All I had to do was put the bow lines onto the main trolling poles next to the main line and the pig line. A lot of boats had been set up that way if they didn't have bow poles. If it didn't work out, I could always put them back on for next season.

I'd have to keep the licence number painted on the side, but no need to have the name on the side of the boat. Well, legally, yes, but it wouldn't be noticed. A bit of gray paint over the name and the Hawkeye would be just another fish boat. Anyone looking at it from the side would assume the name was on the stern and anyone looking for it on the stern would assume it was on the sides. Nobody would question it.

I'd also add a dodger to the top of the wheelhouse. The new raised rim around the roof would help change the look of the boat; make it look taller like one of those fancy fibreglass boats. By the time I was through with the changes, it wouldn't look anything like the old Hawkeye and with the gray paint job, it would blend right into the sea. I'd be like a ghost ship, prowling on the misty horizon. *Now you see me—now you don't. But I'll see YOU. I'll be watching you, Serenity, watching for my chance, and you won't even know it.*

I grinned as I drove off the ferry and headed for the marine supply store. My headache was history and I had a plan. They weren't going to get old Robert down that easily. If they thought they'd seen the last of me, they were in for a surprise. My plan would be more aggressive and slick now. Fucking wife stealer. I'm coming to reclaim my Andrea. I rubbed my hands together. Revenge would be cruel and sweet.

Chapter 23

I had mixed feelings about our Hawaii plans. All I had wanted was to get Andrea safely out of Robert's reach. I hadn't been to Hawaii in years—never really wanted to spend much time there with all the tourist crowds—but it was a quick and affordable fix for the situation we were in. We could enjoy some warmth and sunshine, eat healthy, and most importantly get away from that lunatic.

I had called Giselle. "You're going to shoot me after I ask this big favour of you."

"I doubt it, Jim. You know I'd do anything for you. What's up?"

"I need to get Andrea away from here until Robert cools his heels. I thought I'd take her to Hawaii for a couple of months, maybe longer."

"And you want me to check on the house? Of course. I know what to do. Say no more. Just make your arrangements and let me know when you're leaving."

Thank God for Giselle. "You're a doll, Giselle."

"I know," she said. I could imagine her smiling through the phone. "And would you like Jacques to check on the boat while you're away? You know, check the bilge, make sure there's no extra water, check the rubber bumpers, check the ropes...?"

"I was going to ask. You think he wouldn't mind?"

"Of course not. After you make your arrangements, we'll meet you at the wharf before you go and you can show us exactly what you want us to do."

I was so lucky to have those two friends. I felt confident leaving things in their care. I just hoped that Robert wouldn't come around and make any trouble for them.

In the departure lounge of the Comox airport, Andrea and I sat with about fifty other people, anxiously awaiting our final boarding call.

Andrea was chewing her fingernails. "You look worried." I mimicked her chewing action. She whipped her fingers out of her mouth. "It's not too late to change our minds," I said. "We could stay home and be cozy in front of the fire this winter, read, go to movies, entertain...."

"Nice try, but I'll stick to the Hawaii plan." She drummed her fingers on her carry-on bag. "Nervous flyer. But I'll be fine."

We sat in silence for a few minutes, people watching. "Did you remember to give Giselle the key?" she asked.

"Giselle always has a key. She and Jacques are my standby people. Don't worry. They'll look after the place."

"There's not that much to do, really, is there?"

"Nothing at all, but for the insurance to be valid, someone has to check the place regularly. Giselle has been doing that for me for years when I'm away fishing or on a holiday."

"You're lucky to have good friends like that. Like Monique is for me."

"Yes, I am." I leaned over to give her a peck on the cheek. "And now I have one more."

I feel like I'm already on a holiday just being safe from Robert. It's so wonderful to know that he can't suddenly show up and it's just you and me," she said. "Just imagine if our whole lives could be like this—Robert-less."

"That's my goal. To shake him loose." I gave her hand a squeeze. "That's why I thought this trip to Hawaii might be a good idea. I know it was a bit sudden, but I think it's just what we need."

"Right now I feel like I'd like to stay there forever, just to be away from him."

"Well, we can stay a lot longer by going to Kauai rather than booking an expensive hotel in Honolulu. When we land we can just catch the shuttle bus to the smaller airport and fly right on to Kauai."

Andrea shrugged. "Sure. But why did you pick Kauai?"

"It's cheap to live there in a campsite. Giselle and Jacques have been there and they gave me a few tips on where to go and what to do."

When we came out of the air-conditioned Honolulu airport, the heat and humidity walloped us. The whole place was one big sauna and my clothes were a hot wet blanket. Lugging the suitcases across the traffic lanes to the boulevard where the crowded WikiWiki bus stopped, I was soon drenched in sweat. I followed Andrea onto the bus shoving the luggage ahead of me. My feet were barely aboard, wedged in between the suitcases, when the driver took off. I felt sorry for Andrea. She had the misfortune of having her nose at another standee's sweaty armpit level as he held onto a pole. I tugged at

Andrea's upper arm. "Here, sit down on the bags." She sank down gratefully.

"Almost there," I said.

Andrea gave me a wilted smile and nodded.

Oh God! This is only the beginning. The heat, the people. Oh, to be alone on my boat riding the cool waves right now ... except it's October and the winter storms are raging back home.

Chapter 24

Over the past few weeks, I made the changes to my boat and left it at Finn Bay, out of sight. Few people would know that this was the Hawkeye, and those who did, wouldn't care. I now had time to go back and forth to Comox as I wanted. As an extra precaution, I got a few cans of spray paint and drove the truck out into the bush one day. Later that night, my mint green truck was a dull charcoal colour. I'd even let my hair grow a bit longer. New boat, new truck, new me. My whole image was now changed.

By December I figured the cops had calmed down about me staying on the Powell River side of the Strait of Georgia. I packed up some camping gear for sleeping in the back of the truck and headed for the island.

It was quiet at Jim's house, so I went down to the Comox wharf. It was windy and raining sideways so I figured no one would recognize me all bundled up with the hood up on my jacket. The few people I met had their head down and were bent over to avoid the weather.

One fellow who lived on his sailboat came out on his deck when he saw me looking through the windows of the Serenity.

"Looking for someone?" he asked.

I turned on the charm and introduced myself. "My name's Tom. I'm a friend of Jim's. Is he around?"

The sailboat guy shook his head. "No, he's in Hawaii, lucky bugger."

"Really!? He didn't say anything about it last time I talked to him."

"That must have been a while. They've been gone since late October."

"They?"

"Yeah, him and Andrea."

Damn! "Oh that's too bad." *What a piss off. On the other hand, that gives me free rein on my plans.*

"What do you mean, 'that's too bad'?" He reached back through the cabin door and grabbed his rain jacket.

"Oh!" *Careful! Don't let your inner feelings come out.* "I meant that's too bad because I've missed him again."

"Where'd you say you knew him from?"

"I didn't say, but I know him from fishing up north years ago. I live in Nanaimo now." It was always good to pair up lies with a little truth. Keep them from getting suspicious.

"So they've gone to Hawaii. Son of a gun." I grinned like a fool. "I'm sorry to have missed him. He say how long they'd be gone?"

The guy pulled the hood of his rain jacket tighter at his throat to keep the wind and rain out. "Nope, but with this shit weather we're having, I hope it's a good long time. They deserve a nice long break."

"Well, thanks for filling me in. I'm in Comox once in a while so I'll pop down to the wharf now and then when I'm in town and just check to see if they're back yet." *And that way if you happen to see me messing around with the boat, you won't send out the troops.*

Chapter 25

Kauai with Jim was a dream. We'd been here for three months and I never tired of it. After all the misery I endured with Robert last year, I would never have believed I could feel so healthy and happy again. Swimming, eating lots of fruit and vegetables, sightseeing in our rent-a-wreck car, walking the beaches, hiking trails—it was the perfect holiday. And I was with a man I loved.

Our accommodations were rustic to say the least. It was only a partially closed in shelter with a thatched roof, but in this great climate we didn't need more. A couple of metal spring beds stood in the middle of the room. We pushed them together and covered the stained mattresses with plastic. The small counter had a gas barbecue for outdoor cooking, under a bit of an extension of the roof in case of rain.

The campsite was up on a high hill, out of the way of most of the tourist traffic. The peaceful atmosphere was just what we needed. I'd had many months of the silence of desperate loneliness and misery when Robert had kept me isolated in our cabin last year, but what Jim and I had here was the quiet of contentment and companionship.

The sky was often overcast. It took us a while to figure out that, just because it was cloudy over our campsite, it didn't mean the sun wasn't shining at the beach a few miles down the hill. We had stayed in our camp for the first three days waiting for the sun to appear. Finally we decided to go into town, down at sea level, for something to do. What a surprise when we realized it was hot and sunny down there. That was often the case and we learned to work with the weather.

I was lying in my lounge chair outside our palapa, reading a romance novel I'd picked up in town when Jim pulled in with the car. He plunked down two bags of groceries on the counter beside the barbecue.

"I think we should celebrate tonight." He pulled out two big steaks. "I'll barbecue the steaks and maybe you could make up a salad to go with them?"

"Sure...." I put my book down. "What are we celebrating?"

"Our time in Hawaii, and maybe our plans to go home soon?" Jim raised his eyebrows, waiting for my answer.

"You want to go home?" *I guess I knew the time would have to come.*

"I think it's soon time." He pulled up the lawn chair close to my lounge chair. "I have to start thinking about doing some maintenance on the boat and getting it ready to go fishing soon."

Funny that he was looking forward to going home, while for me, a black cloud moved into my brain. My head began to pound with an instant stress headache. "Of course you do." I patted his hand and tried to smile, but I couldn't shake the image of Robert lurking everywhere, ready to grab me and take me back to a life of seclusion and punishment.

Chapter 26

Andrea seemed subdued since we packed our things and left Kahili Mountain Park. On our way to the airport, I had an idea.

"I know you're not thrilled about going home—"

"Oh, no, it's not that. I love your home and it'll be nice to be in Comox again, but … well.…"

I patted her thigh as we drove along. "I'm sure Robert will have given up by now."

She inhaled deeply and hunched up her shoulders. "You don't know how strong-willed he can be. He'll never quit." She blew out the breath she'd been holding and quickly added, "But it's been really nice here. A relaxing, beautiful break from all those troubles."

"I have an idea. We have until the day after tomorrow to catch that flight back to Comox, so there are a couple of places I'd like to show you before we head home."

We rented a different car from Rent-a-Wreck in Honolulu and some distance out of town, we booked into a motel. "This is a little bit cheaper than right in the city. You don't mind, do you?"

"Are you kidding me? After camping for four months this is luxury."

"Let's go pick up a few things from the grocery store and take a picnic to the beach."

"Not Waikiki again," she said. "I was so disappointed when we stopped there for our quick walk this morning.

I bet there was a cigarette butt every ten inches in every direction."

"Yeah, that poor guy trying to sweep the beach clean.... Good luck to him. Those butts eventually fall apart but the filters are there for a long time. Not a place I'd want to place my beach mat for a lengthy stay."

Andrea had picked up a tourist pamphlet from the motel room desk. "Do you know any other place else we could go?"

"I sure do. There's a place I went with my dad a long time ago."

"Where's that?"

I grinned at her. "Secret." She pulled a face. "Come on. We need our masks and fins and snorkels."

Andrea high-fived me and hustled over to the bags to sort out our swimming and snorkeling gear.

We stopped at a grocery store and filled our cart with an assortment of our favourite foods. With our bags of fresh pineapple, a couple of mangos, a papaya, a bag of chips, and a couple of bottles of water loaded into the back of the car, we drove farther out of Honolulu, along the beach. I turned in where the sign said, "Hanauma Bay."

"You're going to love snorkeling here. The fish, the plants, the coral—oh, speaking of which, there are some kinds of coral you shouldn't touch."

"Why not?"

"Actually, it's not a real coral but it looks like a seaweed-shaped coral. The little organisms on it have tiny tentacles that give you a stinging feeling like a jellyfish sting if you touch it."

Andrea made a face. "Eek! I've never even heard of it. Thanks for telling me."

"Hanauma Bay is full of coral reefs and rocks—that's why the fish are so plentiful there—and I thought you might not know about fire coral. Coming from Ontario and all." I smiled as I remembered how naïve she was when I first met her and she was a real landlubber, helping me scrub the bottom of the boat. She knew less than nothing about the sea then.

"I'm sure I'll be fine. I just won't go hugging any rock walls that look like they're covered in fire coral."

We put our beach mat down and got our snorkeling equipment out. "You okay with a swim first and a snack later?" I asked her.

"Can't wait to get in the water and cool off."

We waded into the bay. The shallow part of the bay near the beach was alive with people snorkeling and floating. "I'm going to head out a little farther," I said. "You just poke around wherever you feel comfortable. I won't be far away. Don't go out too far, will you?"

"I'll just be right here."

I headed for the deeper water at the sheltered side of the bay, where I could at least snorkel without getting someone's flipper in the face. I gave Andrea a wave and left her in the shallower water. She'd be fine there.

Chapter 27

The ocean was the perfect temperature, the sand in the shallows soothing on my feet. When I got in past my knees, I waded a little more hoping for deeper water before getting in completely, but the slope had leveled out and thigh deep was as good as it got. No wonder there were so many kids and their parents splashing around with shrieks of, "Look at this, Mom," and "Dad, Dad, come here. Get a load of this purple fish." I could understand why Jim had been in a hurry to get to deeper water.

I wasn't a strong swimmer, but I could swim well enough, so I thought that somewhere in between the kiddie pool and Jim's deeper water was a good place for me. Jim had gone way over on the far side of the bay, not too far out, but just away from all the kids. I was disappointed that he didn't stay near me while we snorkeled, but I could understand him wanting to get away from the crowds. He wasn't used to having a lot of people around like I was—at least that's how it used to be when I lived in Ontario. It's what I was trying to get away from when I came out west—all that busy downtown hubbub. Well, I got more isolation than I bargained for when I married Robert. But Jim and I had been practically glued together for the past few months, so I couldn't blame him for wanting some alone time.

Once I got beyond the crowd near shore, I slipped into the water and let it float me around wherever it wanted to take me. Once in a while, I moved my flippers gently, and watched the world go by. The water world, that is. The fish didn't seem to mind me being there. It must be that they were used to so many tourists being in the water here, day after day, year after year. It was a park, after all.

Tiny purple fish swam past. Zebra stripes, brilliant electric blue, bulgy-eyed, gold with streamer-like fins, black and yellow, flat ones parallel to the bottom, flat ones perpendicular to the bottom, some with moustaches sweeping the bottom, tiny neon types—aquarium escapees. I was fascinated watching their actions—inquisitive, floating, flitting, hunting, wary. I followed one fish that was about two feet long if you didn't count the needle-like tail that added on another eight inches or so. It had a face that looked like its lips would attach to my mask and never let go, but it swam near the bottom so I didn't think I'd have a problem with it. It looked like a candle or a pipe and I made a mental note to look it up when we got home. The fish hid in the plant life or in mini caves within the coral, which I didn't touch, just in case. The reef seemed to go for quite some distance like the wall of a swimming pool. I followed along the wall and when I came to an opening I floated through it easily. The fish on the other side of the wall were slightly bigger and there were fewer of them, but still, enough to be entertaining.

After a while, I lifted my head to look for Jim, but he was no longer in the deeper area where he had first gone. I scanned the shallow bay and thought I saw him standing in the middle of the rabble. I decided it was a good time to come in, so I kicked my flippers towards the opening in the reef, intending to go through it back to the shallow pool. The water wasn't deep here on the other side, but over my head just the same.

As I reached the entrance to the sheltered bay, I kicked to go through it, but the sea sucked me backwards into the deeper water again. When that wave was gone and a new one headed for shore, I kicked hard to go through the opening this time. I was halfway through when the wave receded again and took me back with it. I needed to hang onto something so I wouldn't be swept back next time, but there was only the reef, and I had Jim's warning in my head. *Don't touch the fire coral.*

The wave had taken me out again and I turned to look out towards the deeper water of the open sea behind me. The headland of the bay was shaped like a lion guarding a gate. Would I end up there? I turned to look for Jim. He had his arm up shading his eyes from the sun, looking for me among so many heads in the bay. He didn't know I was way out here.

I kicked to get back to the gap in the coral reef, but by the time I reached it the next wave was already taking me out again. My muscles were burning and tired and I tried not to panic, but my stomach clenched as invading waves of fear washed over me. I had three choices: yell for help, embarrassing and no one would hear me anyway; hold onto the coral and maybe get stung—if I could get to the entrance again, that is; or be swept out to that headland where I'm sure the sharks were already smacking their lips as they cruised back and forth. None of those choices appealed to me.

Someplace deep inside of me, there had to be a reserve of energy. I reminded myself that I was no longer the helpless Andrea who had let herself be beaten and cowed. I was the new Andrea with guts and determination. When the next wave took me close to the gap in the reef, I went with it and then kicked and kicked with all my might while the surge threatened to take me back out. I only had to keep up the super hard kicking for another few seconds before another wave would push me in again. *Hang in there.* At last, the wave came and I imagined Robert's fists pounding me. I kicked away from him and that extra burst of energy took me into the shelter of the bay. I looked up again and Jim had spotted me. He waved, smiling. I waved, smiling. Little did he know my whole body was shaking. I lay face down in the water again and slowly snorkeled in very close to shore, only getting up to walk when the water was knee deep because I couldn't trust my legs to carry me.

Jim came rushing over. "Andrea! I didn't know where you were." He grabbed my upper arms when I teetered off balance. "I should have stayed with you, but after so much time together I thought you'd be happy for a break from me."

"Never," I gasped.

Jim turned to look at my face. "Hey! Are you okay?"

"Sure am." *Now.* "What do you say to a bit of lunch? Pineapple?" I coughed to mask my quavering voice.

As we left the beach later on, we stopped by the park gates to look at the huge sign that had a map of the bay posted. "Look here, Jim. It has each area identified. You should never have been swimming where you went. It says 'Dangerous Undertow.'"

"So it does! And where were you swimming?"

I looked on the map. The whole area where I had gone through the gap said, "Strong swimmers only."

I waved in the general direction of the safe side of the reef. "Oh, somewhere around here."

I took Jim's arm and walked to the car with him. "Come on. I'm good and ready to go home." I knew Robert would be waiting for me somewhere and sometime soon, but after today I could face anything.

Chapter 28

Jacques and Giselle were waiting for Andrea and me at the Comox airport when our afternoon flight arrived from Vancouver. Hawaii had been great, but it was sure good to be home and see the smiling faces of my good friends. I hugged Giselle and shook Jacques' hand.

"Man, look at you! So brown!" Jacques stood back to admire our tans.

"I feel anemic," Giselle said. "But no matter, you both look like you had a wonderful holiday. Lots of sun anyway."

"It really was fantastic." Andrea wrapped her arms around herself and shivered.

"I brought you each a jacket from your own closest just to warm you up a little until you get home." Giselle handed over the jackets she had bundled under one arm.

"I have to admit, I'm glad to have this just now. Thanks, Giselle." I'd been shivering too since we landed in Vancouver earlier today.

"I guess it will take a while to get used to our cool weather. But don't worry. It will soon be spring." Giselle took Andrea's carry-on bag. "Here, let me. The guys can get the suitcases."

"You go on out to the car, Giselle, and warm it up," Jacques said. "I'll follow with Jim when the baggage arrives." He turned to me then and muttered, "I have to talk to you about the boat."

My stomach tightened. "What's up?"

"Nothing so bad I had to call you to come home, but funny little things...."

I could feel my brow furrowing and frown wrinkles forming. "Like what?"

"Well, you know I went to check on the boat every two days or so, and always after it rained or blew."

"Yeah." *Come on, Jacques. Spit it out!* My fingers drummed on the sides of my legs.

"A couple of times I went down there and the ropes were tied differently."

Whew! Is that all? "Oh, don't worry about that. The wharfinger probably just retied them. He goes around and checks the ropes when he's bored."

Jacques shook his head and waved away my explanations. "He would know how to tie the ropes properly. The ropes were loose."

"They do sometimes work loose a bit when it's been bad weather," I said.

"No. This was too strange. They were all loosened a lot and then made to look like they were still tied. It was a good thing I was down there or the next big wind would have taken the boat away from the dock and God knows where it would have ended up."

That is a bit strange. "Weird. Well, it's good you spotted it. Thanks a lot." *Robert?*

"But that's not all," Jacques said. "Another time I was down there, your rigging lines were dangling and I know you always have them tightly secured on the belaying pins. Your poles could have come crashing down and broken, not to mention smashing the boat tied next to yours."

"Holy shit," I muttered under my breath. *Fucking asshole.*

"And another time I checked and all the bumpers had been lifted aboard so your boat was rubbing up against the one next to you. There's a bit of damage where the other guy's boat rubbed a spot, but your guard saved you from more damage."

"Jesus," I whispered. Alarm bells were ringing. *Robert's been busy. I wonder what other damage he's done.*

"So I started coming to the wharf more often just in case. Is there someone in town who doesn't like you?" Jacques asked, laughing uncomfortably.

"There's crazy Robert," I said, "but he's not supposed to be here. He was told to leave town after he tried to snatch Andrea."

"Whatever happened about that?"

"The police couldn't prove anything and, as they are married, he wasn't kidnapping her. Gave him a warning about his behaviour and sent him back to Powell River."

"I wonder if he's back here in Comox," Jacques said. "Bill—you know Bill from the sailboat—he said some guy from Nanaimo had been looking for you. Said his name was Tom."

"Hmm ... I don't know any Tom from Nanaimo. I wonder if he looked like Robert."

"Why don't you ask Bill what he looked like?"

"Yeah, I think I will." *I bet he was tall and big and dark haired.*

"Something's not right there. You'd better keep a close watch on that boat."

I nodded. "And Andrea." *Shit! Welcome home.*

Chapter 29

I didn't tell Andrea what Jacques had said about the boat. We settled in at home as quickly as we could, and while Andrea unpacked I made arrangements to take the boat to Nanaimo to get hauled out at the shipyard there in April. They were already getting booked up. There was pressure to book early, but the whole venture would be a waste of money if it pissed down rain all week while I had the boat out of the water. I hoped the weather would co-operate, but it was always a crap shoot. April could be pretty wet on the island, but if it rained, I could at least get the hull work done. I'd just have to do the painting of the parts above the waterline at the wharf in Comox once we got a few sunny days.

When April rolled around, Andrea was a big help preparing and packing the things we needed for the ten-day trip. Traveling to and from Nanaimo would only be part of it, because we had to live on the boat at the shipyard for the week we were working on the hull.

"We could do it in one long run," I said, "but I think it will be more fun if we only go as far as French Creek and stay overnight there before continuing on to Nanaimo the next day."

"That sounds good," Andrea said. "I've got most of our clothes packed. Just need to get the food together and check your list for any odds and ends. You're taking care of the tools, right?"

"Yup! I think we're as good as ready to go. We'll just get a few fresh veggies tomorrow and maybe a bottle of wine. It's only a few hours to French Creek, so we'll leave as soon as we get our shopping done."

It felt good to pull away from the wharf. All my troubles, not that I had any big ones except Robert, were left behind. If there was anything I had forgotten to load onto the boat, it was too late to worry about it now. I had my satellite phone in case of emergency, but really, everything I needed was on the boat—food, water, Andrea. I glanced over at her as she sat in the passenger seat at the front of the wheelhouse. She looked content. Like me, she was probably happy to pull away from shore and all those Robert troubles. She hadn't talked about getting a job anymore since Hawaii. I hoped I had convinced her that there was no rush. I would pay her deckhand wages and she could build up her own bank account that way.

It was sunny, but a cool breeze from the north put a slight chop on the water. Not too bad though, because the tide was with us as we headed south. We were making good time. I scanned the waters in front of us—no traffic—and then the horizon. Just a sailboat on its way to somewhere, and a Seaspan tug across the strait toward the Vancouver side, towing a barge with a huge load of containers stacked on it. Behind me I saw no one except a distant small boat. Port and starboard looked clear. Smooth sailing ahead.

"Wanna make us a pot of coffee?" I called to Andrea as I settled into the captain's bench at the helm.

Andrea hung her jacket on a hook. I admired her trim figure. She answered my eyebrow lifts with a big smile. "Sure thing, Cap'n." I watched her as she pushed the kettle to the hotter part of the stove and spooned coffee into the filter on top of the coffeepot.

She busied herself tidying up the galley while I fiddled with the Nobeltec program and plotted our waypoints. Once I had the waypoints entered, the boat could be on autopilot and pretty much take us to French Creek by itself. We just had to watch for obstructions in the water, like logs or other boats.

Andrea brought me a cup of coffee with a tiny bit of Demerara sugar in it, just the way I like it. I put my arm around her waist and pulled her close. "This reminds me of the time you and Monique made the trip from Lund to Comox with me." I set my coffee on the helm and nuzzled her hair.

"I already loved you then, and I love you more than ever now." I stood up and hugged her, and kissed her sweet lips.

"I figured it was something like that," she said.

"What do you mean?"

She pressed herself into me and wiggled her hips back and forth. "Your body tells me you're not lying."

I chuckled and pulled her into me tighter. "But I think I could be lying…."

I had to laugh at her suddenly serious look. "Yes, I could be lying. We could both be lying." I glanced around at the water—all clear—looked at the instrumentation— all set up and on track—and added, "Yup! We could, and I think we should." I pulled her over to the bunk in the galley. I'd have to make it a quickie, but my hands in her pants told me I didn't think she'd mind. She was ready for me.

I pulled Andrea's jeans partway down, but she insisted on taking them off. "I need my legs free to wrap around you." She was quick to help me get mine off as well. I thanked the builder of the Serenity for making the bunk nice and wide. He was a big fellow and insisted on comfort. It served us well today. I made love to Andrea gently and yet urgently. Didn't know that was possible, but I loved her as much as I wanted her. She wrapped her legs around mine and held on like vise grips while she pushed herself against me. I disappeared into her completely. She groaned and I pulled back. "No! Don't pull away."

"I don't want to hurt you."

She pulled with her locked legs and her arms around my back. "You won't." I rocked inside her and felt her gripping me with every part of her body, down to the muscles in her most tender parts. Andrea's stifled squeal released my groan of pleasure when I filled her up and we collapsed, spent, on the bunk.

"Oops!" I jumped up and ran to the helm, looking around.

"What is it?" Andrea asked.

"Nothing. Just haven't checked where we were going for a bit."

Andrea giggled.

"What?"

"I like the captain's outfit," she said.

I stepped into my jeans, smiling to think she liked what she saw. I liked what I saw too. She looked great, her hair tousled from that roll in the hay. Was I lucky or what?

"What're you grinning about?" she asked as she wiggled into her jeans. She came up to stand beside me at the helm and leaned into me.

My hand slid over her hips and I pulled her close to me for a kiss. "I was just thinking what a lucky guy I am to have you here with me."

"That makes two of us," she said. "When I think of what my life was like only a year ago...."

"Don't think about it."

"Sometimes it's hard to get it all out of my head; it was such a nightmare." She kissed my cheek as I climbed back into the captain's bench behind the wheel. "Thank God for you." She shook her head slowly. "I thought I'd be trapped with him forever. Can you imagine how depressing that was? I couldn't see any way out. Can hardly believe I'm here with you and my life is good again."

"So is mine," I said. I reached for my coffee cup up on the helm, took a slurp, and made a face. "Coffee's cold. Do you mind pouring me another cup? I think there's box of cookies in the cupboard under the sink."

"Ooh! Cookies!" She turned to go fix the coffee.

I checked for boats again. It was a natural reflex to glance around every few minutes whenever I was running the boat. "Look out the door and let me know if you see any boat traffic behind us, eh?"

She leaned out the door to the deck and looked towards the stern. "Just one tiny gray boat way in the distance."

Chapter 30

The light was fading as we neared the entrance to French Creek. Andrea had been on the wheel. "I want to get back into practice for this season," she said.

"Check the monitor," I told her. "See the entrance?"

"Yup, I see it." She started angling the boat towards shore.

"Not yet," I said.

"But I can see the entrance right here, and if I don't start turning, we'll miss it."

I zoomed in on the map on the monitor and pointed at the path she was planning to take. "If you go in here, you'll take us up the creek, and all the paddles in the world won't save us." She hurried to correct the heading and turned us away from land again. "Look," I said, "this first indentation is the creek—French Creek—and around that spit that comes out farther ahead, that's where you go in for the boat basin. See it here?"

"Oh ... my...." She clapped a hand over her mouth. "I could have run us aground."

"Don't worry. I was watching too. It's an easy mistake though, and you always have to look at the whole picture."

"Sorry!"

"Don't worry about it. It's getting too dark to see the entrance, but on the Nobeltec map you can see it on the monitor. So go ahead and bring us in now. I'll take it when we get near the floats." She did all right then, and

I finished off the last bit of maneuvering. Since there was no dockside space, I brought the Serenity next to another troller that was tied to the dock. "Throw a line around her poles," I called to Andrea, who already stood with our midship line in her hand.

We shut the engine down and both of us sighed and then laughed. "Feels good to shut it down, doesn't it?" I said.

She nodded. "You don't realize how noisy it is and how you've tuned out the sound of the engine until you shut it off."

I cupped my ear. "Eh?"

Andrea raised her voice. "I said you don't realize—" She stopped when she saw me grinning, and punched my arm.

"Some old-timer told me once that these engines run quieter every year. You fish long enough you don't even hear them at all."

"I can see how that could happen. That constant engine noise must do some damage to your hearing when you're around it so much."

I pulled up a corner of the carpet on the floor and pointed. "And this is with extra underlay to insulate the wheelhouse from the engine noise.

"Here, we'd better plug in to shore power now or our freezer is going to thaw. You go outside and I'll pass you the cord through the window. Plug it in to the pole with the power outlets down there." I pushed the side window open a crack for the cord to fit through.

I turned down the diesel stove so it was on low, just enough to keep the chill off the wheelhouse. I checked the gauges and flipped a few switches off. Everything seemed to be running fine. Not bad for the first day's run.

"I think that's it then. Let's grab a jacket and head up to the restaurant. I'll treat you to dinner."

We walked up the ramp to the parking lot and I took one last look back to check on the boat. Way down at the far end of the floats was the gray boat that had been behind us all day. I didn't know the boat, but I couldn't shake the feeling that there was something familiar about it.

Chapter 31

The restaurant wasn't really fancy, but it was better than the pub on the lower floor. Jim chose a table near the window where we had a view of the water—not that we needed to look at more water. Still it was romantic and we had a good meal.

"I'm really looking forward to us fishing together this summer," Jim said. "It gets kind of boring sometimes and it'll be nice to have you there. A lot more fun."

"I hope so. We won't be bored, but it's a very small space…." I knew all about being confined in small spaces after a summer on Robert's boat, but this would be different. "As long as we get along."

"Of course we'll get along. You just have to do as you're told." Jim gave me a wink.

"That's what Robert used to say too." I shivered.

Jim reached across the table for my hand. "Aw, that's not fair. It's not the same."

I winced. *Why did I have to say that?* "I know. Of course it's not the same. It's going to take a while to get all those 'Robertisms' out of my head. Sorry."

"We'll make new memories," Jim said. "Good ones."

We talked about plans for fishing that summer and how we would make the trip north a real holiday. "We can leave a few weeks earlier than usual and have that extra time to dawdle our way north," he said. "There are so many beautiful places on the coast."

I had seen glimpses of some of the pristine bays and inlets along the amazing B.C. coast when I was with Robert last spring, but it wasn't much of a picnic then. He was in a hurry to get to the fishing grounds off the Charlottes and had no time or interest in visiting scenic places along the way. No appreciation for the wonders of nature. This time, it would be different. "It's going to be fabulous. I just know it."

Jim raised my hand to his lips. "I can hardly wait to get going this year. So much to look forward to. No more lonely times on the boat."

"Do you get lonely?" I asked. Somehow I always thought only women got lonely.

Jim made some funny mumbling noises with his mouth, shrugged one shoulder, and finally said, "Mmwell, yeah. Sometimes."

"That's okay. Good to know you're human." Men! They were so silly sometimes, especially when they were asked about their feelings.

"When you're fishing, the days get pretty long. Boring too. So it'll be nice if we can each have a catnap while the other keeps a watch on things. Lack of sleep is one of the worst parts of fishing. Those summer daylight hours seem to go on forever when you're so far north. Never enough time for sleep."

"I think there will be a whole variety of benefits to being together on the boat."

"I can think of a few right now." Jim got that mischievous look on his face. A look I was beginning to recognize and love. "We'll get the Serenity in shape this week at the shipyard and next week when we're finished, we'll make a quick stop at home for a few days to get the house together and to buy the groceries we need. Then we can take off for a holiday and work our way north. We won't worry about fishing until it's nearly time to start."

We shared a piece of cheesecake for dessert and Jim smiled at me across the table. "We'll have a great summer," he said. "We'll take our time getting up there and then we'll have a good season. Life is good." He stood up and held up my jacket for me to slip into. "And now let's go check out that bunk in the Serenity."

We strolled down to the dock, arm in arm. I hadn't felt so happy even in Hawaii. We had a plan and we were in love. Life was perfect. What more could we ask?

We stepped onto the deck of the Serenity and Jim stopped short. "That's odd. The door's open. I know I locked it." He looked around the deck. Apparently everything was okay. He shrugged and shook his head. "I'm sure I locked it." Inside, everything seemed normal, except for the window that had been open a crack for the cord to go through. "The window's wide open!" Jim stood at the helm and looked out at the other boats. All was quiet.

Then I heard Jim's sharp intake of breath and he reached to grab something from the light over the compass on the helm. He threw open the door to the fo'c'sle and looked to left and right in the downstairs area.

I came up behind him, almost bumping into him as he turned. "What is it?" I whispered.

He stood without speaking or moving. "Jim, you're scaring me. What's wrong?"

He let out a big sigh. "I guess it's not fair not to let you see it. I didn't want you to worry, but...."

I grabbed Jim's hand and pulled it towards me. "What is it?"

Slowly, Jim opened his hand.

I stuffed my fist into my mouth to stifle a scream. I sank down to sit on the bunk. In his hand, Jim held the amulet my mother had given me. I had last seen it on Robert's boat, just before I made my escape last fall.

My body trembled and I dropped my head into my hands. I grasped bunches of my hair tightly in my fists. "Oh my God!" I cried. "He'll never give up. He'll never leave me alone." Sobs came uncontrollably now and waves of fear juddered through me.

Chapter 32

I locked the window and told Andrea to lock the door to the wheelhouse after I went out. "I'm just going to check the dock. I'll be right back. You'll be fine with the door locked."

I looked carefully at every boat on our finger and the next one, but saw nothing suspicious about them. "Huh! That's funny." *The gray boat is gone.*

Odd for someone to come in and tie up and then head out again after dark. Oh well. Maybe he was tired and just needed to have a nap before traveling on. Or ... it was Robert and he'd made a lot of changes to his boat.

I went back to the Serenity, puzzled by the amulet showing up like that. I had last seen it the day I stopped at Robert's cabin to check on Andrea. She wasn't there. Gone home to Ontario, Robert said. The cabin's ashes were still smouldering, and Andrea's amulet was hanging on the compass light in the Hawkeye's wheelhouse. I remember thinking then that she wouldn't have left for Ontario without it.

Robert had to be around somewhere to have brought back the amulet. My neck hair prickled, knowing he might be watching me this very moment, but I'd have to play it down so Andrea wouldn't freak out.

"Nothing to worry about, Andrea. I checked both fingers of the wharf and it's all quiet and normal."

She let out a sigh, but her grimace of fear told me she wasn't ready to let her guard down.

"I didn't want to mention it," I said, "but I wondered about the gray boat that was behind us. It was tied at the end of the wharf when we went up to the restaurant, but it's gone now."

"You think it could have been Robert? But his boat is orange."

"He could have painted it." I gave a half-hearted shrug. "Anyway, if it was him, he's gone now."

I made a pot of Sleepytime Tea and poured us each a cup. I sat beside Andrea on the bunk next to the fold-down table and put my arm around her. I pulled her close to me and kissed her head.

"I'm here and I won't let him get you. You sleep right here in my bunk with me and nobody will hurt you."

She sniffed and wiped her nose with the tissue I handed her. "Okay." She was still shaking. "Can we lock the door?"

"Sure can. And I'll re-check the wedges in the sliding windows of the wheelhouse so no one can push them open." I got up and pulled the curtains closed, shutting out any possibility of peeping eyes.

Andrea sat, quietly alert, listening and getting up to peek out between the curtains every time she heard a noise.

"Just some fisherman going to check his boat," I said.

"Could be Robert," she said. "He's got to be around somewhere."

"He's gone," I said. "I'm sure he's gone. I really think that was his boat at the end of the dock. He's gone."

It took a while before she was calm enough to crawl into the bunk with me.

"I'm so scared," she whispered.

"Don't worry. He's done his little stunt and now he's run away."

Andrea shuddered, her fist clenched around a fold of my T-shirt. "He'll be back."

I knew she was right.

Chapter 33

The morning stillness at the French Creek wharf was broken by the cry of seagulls shrieking and squawking on the breakwater. Jim rolled out and sat on the edge of the bed, running his hands through his hair, his usual way of waking up. I propped myself up on my elbow. I stayed in his bunk watching as he went to the front of the wheelhouse and flipped a couple of switches. The Serenity's diesel engine sprang to life. Such a rude noise so early in the morning.

He must have noticed my frown. "I like it to warm up a while before we head out."

"Why is that?" I asked. "It can warm up all the way to Nanaimo." I smiled.

"Ha, ha. Very funny."

I swung my legs out of bed and groped for my clothes. "But really, what does it matter?"

Jim explained as he got dressed. "Better for the engine to give the oil a chance to circulate, and makes for quicker response time when I need to change gears. When you're around other boats, like here at the wharf, you have to maneuver back and forth, and you need the boat to respond right away or you could run into another boat. And anyway, it's not good for the engine if you make a habit of starting out cold all the time."

"Oh. I didn't know that. I thought it was just a bunch of metal." I pulled on my jeans and poked my arms into a sweatshirt to wear over my T-shirt. It was still cool in the mornings and would be cooler out on the water, but when I shivered it was at the memory of Robert being on the boat while we were out. He was such a snake.

I tried to shake off thoughts of Robert. "I'll make us some coffee. Want some toast?"

"Sure. You can get the coffee started, but I'll get you to untie us when the engine is warm. We can make some breakfast once we're underway."

I sensed that, like me, Jim would be a lot more relaxed once we were away from the dock and on our way to Nanaimo. I liked the idea of being like an unapproachable island. It would be much harder for Robert to get to us on the water than on land.

About ten minutes later, we were out of French Creek's harbour and in the open water. A low streak of mist hung over the water, but it looked like it would be a fine day as soon as the sun rose a little higher in the sky. The Serenity cut smoothly through the slight surface ripple and I was able to pour water through the coffee filter without spilling it.

I brought Jim's coffee to his captain's seat where he was setting up the day's waypoints on the Nobeltec program. What a blessing that computer program was. You always knew exactly where you were and how deep the water was. It gave your speed and how long before you would arrive at your destination. The only thing it didn't do was tell us where Robert was.

"Keep an eye out for boats or logs," Jim said.

I scanned the water. "None that I can see, but I'll keep watching." Today I would be much more on the lookout for a gray boat.

Chapter 34

The small islands in front of Nanaimo looked pristine, pure and untouched, a stark contrast to the built up coast of Vancouver Island behind them. Nanaimo was a busy city. I was torn between awe and disappointment. After the purely natural coastline I had seen on my way north to the Queen Charlotte Islands last year, it was already quite a change to see houses here and there along the beaches south from Comox, but the density of the development in Nanaimo caught me by surprise. Houses spread from the waterfront far up to the hills beyond it.

Not only was there more road traffic, but the water traffic increased as well. Speed boats and small sport fishing boats were everywhere. Jim gripped the wheel and slowed us down to a crawl as we entered the channel between the city and Newcastle Island.

Moments later, the shipyard came in sight. "Here we go," he said with a sigh of relief. "They even have a space for us at their dock."

We tied up the boat and walked up the ramp to check in at the office and let them know we were there.

"When do you think they'll haul us out?" I asked Jim.

"Well, this won't be like Lund, where we got winched out in a cradle that ran on railway tracks in the water. This time they're going to lift us out."

"Lift a big boat like this? You're kidding, right?"

"No, see that big rig there? That's a Travel Lift. They drive it over that space up ahead. It's like a dock with the center piece missing, so they can drive on either edge of the dock. They drop four big wide belts down into the water and then we slide the boat under the Travel Lift and over the belts. They winch up the belts and lift the boat out of the water. They'll drive the Travel Lift over to a space in the parking lot and prop up the boat with timbers."

"If you don't mind, I don't want to be on board when they lift us out of the water."

Jim laughed. "Don't worry. They don't allow anyone to be on the boat while they lift it. We'll wait on the parking lot where they set the boat down."

"It'll sure be a lot easier to work on the boat on the parking lot than it was in Stan's yard, where it was basically propped up on the beach."

"Oh, it's so much better. And it doesn't matter what the tide is doing. We're completely dry the whole time we work on it. Unless it rains. But I mean we're not in the salt water worrying about what the tide is doing."

"I can't wait to get started," I said. "It'll be fun."

With the boat propped up in its place in the shipyard, we set to work.

In my coveralls, I stood looking at the hull of the boat. "Gosh this brings back memories."

Jim laughed. "Not sure I should let you anywhere near that powerwasher."

"You're never going to let me forget that, are you?" I gave Jim a playful punch in the arm. He danced around pretending to hold a piece of caulking between his thumb and forefinger, mimicking me in a squeaky, high voice, "Oh, get a load of this teredo I found."

I looked at the ground, hiding my smirk from him. "Okay, you've had your fun."

Jim put his arms around me. "I was so pissed off when you blasted the caulking out of the boat."

I laid my head on his shoulders and mumbled, "I know. I felt so stupid. How could I mistake the stuffing between the planks for a shipworm?"

"But you were such a trooper, to hang in there and finish the job."

"You don't know how close I was to quitting."

"But you didn't. I was mad at you, and you still didn't give up. I loved that about you—your staying power. You were so determined."

"I'm so glad you didn't send me packing," I said. "We wouldn't be here together now, if you had."

I powerwashed the boat carefully this time. The hull wasn't too bad—a few barnacles and a light coating of that fine, hairy-looking seaweed. It all came off easily with a quick pass of the wand.

I had just put away the powerwasher and taken my gloves off when Joanne, the lady from the shipyard office, came hurrying over to me.

"Phone call for you at the office. Your father is on the line."

"My father?! How does he know where I am?"

"I don't know. I just took the message. He said he'd wait while I came to get you."

"Okay, thanks. Hmpf." I shook my head in disbelief. "It must be important for him to track me down."

"Be right back," I called to Jim. "Phone."

I followed Joanne back to the office. She pointed to the phone. "I'll just go have a smoke break while you talk to your dad." She headed for the door. "Take your time."

"Thanks," I called after her. I picked up the phone she had left lying on the desk. "Hello?"

Nothing.

"Hello? Dad?" Just a dial tone. I looked at the phone, thinking I might need to push a button. I listened again. Nothing. Why would he be calling me anyway? I'd given my parents Giselle's number for emergencies. *Oh God! What if Mom was sick ... or worse?* I had to call Dad back.

I'd ask the office lady to put it on our bill. I dialed quickly. Mom picked up the phone.

"Mom! Are you okay?" I shouted into the phone.

"Of course I'm okay. Why wouldn't I be?" she said. "Why are you yelling? Are you all right? You sound out of breath."

I let out a long sigh. "Oh, thank God!"

"Andrea? What's happening? Where are you?"

"I'm at the shipyard and they told me at the office that Dad was on the phone, but when I picked up, there was no one on the line. I thought maybe you were sick or something."

"No, I'm fine."

"Dad didn't call here?"

"No."

Chapter 35

It had been easy to find out when and where Jim planned to haul out the Serenity this spring, and I was certain that Andrea would be with him. She would be too afraid to stay behind. At least I'd accomplished that much.

I phoned all the haulout facilities nearby and played stupid. "My skipper told me to come help him copper paint but I forgot to write down the dates."

"What's the boat name?"

"The Serenity."

I heard the sound of pages being flicked. "No, I don't have any bookings for the Serenity. Are you sure you have the right shipyard?"

"Oh ... um ... maybe I got the wrong place. Sorry to bother you."

I did that a couple of times and finally I scored at a shipyard in Nanaimo.

"Sure, he's booked for April 17."

"Thanks a lot. You just saved my job for me."

A few days before the 17th, I put my plan into action. I motored over from Lund, anchoring in the bay at Tree Island across from Comox at night, venturing out for day trips closer to Comox to watch for the Serenity to leave. Once I saw the boat leave Comox Harbour, I took my time, kept out of sight, and trailed them down to French Creek.

I hated that I couldn't stick around at the French Creek dock to see Andrea's reaction when she saw the amulet. She would know beyond any doubt that I had been on Jim's boat. So close. In her space. In her head. But at that point, I wouldn't be able to grab her anyway with Jim hovering around her all the time. I would have to be content with knowing that I was getting her rattled with all these messages I was sending her to let her know I was still around and closing in.

In Nanaimo, when I saw the woman come out of the office and head for the shipyard, I ended the call I had just made to her. I hovered near the edge of the parking lot where I had a clear view of the office and the shipyard. In a pinch I could always slip behind the dumpster to hide.

Only a few moments later, Andrea followed the woman back to the office. Even in her copper-paint-besplattered coveralls, she glowed. Still a looker. She'd been so hot in bed when we first got married. Great body on her—athletic, but enough soft curves. The old urges were stirring and I put my hands in my pants pockets to reassure myself that satisfaction wouldn't be far away now.

I casually turned away from the two women and sauntered over behind the dumpster. Once they were inside the office I half walked, half ran to the outer wall of the office beside the washrooms and laundry facilities. I hadn't expected the office girl to come out again so I ducked into the bathroom. But that was no good. I couldn't keep an eye on Andrea from there. Then I realized the office girl didn't know me and I had no reason to hide from her. I eased my Buck pocket knife out of its case on my belt and tucked it into my jacket pocket. I would use it to persuade Andrea to come with me quietly.

Chapter 36

Joanne came back into the office just as I hung up from talking to Mom. "Everything okay?" she asked.

"It was really weird. There was no one on the line so I called home—just put it on our bill, would you—and my mom said no one had called here."

"That's odd. It was definitely a man who called and asked for you by name. He said he was your dad and it was really important that he talk to you."

A creepy feeling came over me. Could it be? Was it possible that Robert was nearby? Maybe he had followed us. It had to have been him at French Creek. No one else could have left the amulet in the wheelhouse. "Oh my God," I whispered. "Robert."

"Are you okay?" Joanne asked. "You look like you might faint. Here sit down."

I sagged into the chair she pulled out for me. "Would you mind walking back to the boat with me, please? I think someone's been following me."

"Of course I'll come with you. If there's anyone out there we'll soon know, but I don't think you need to worry."

You have no idea!

Robert! I thought I'd throw up. "Joanne, on second thought, I'm just going to run into the bathroom for a sec. I'll be fine. Silly of me to be so paranoid anyway. Maybe you can just keep an eye out for me when I head back to the boat?"

"Sure thing, Andrea. You'll be okay."

I ducked into the washroom next door. Nobody was around except a man just going into the men's room. I went on into the ladies', locking the door behind me.

Chapter 37

I fingered the knife in my jacket pocket. It would only take me a second to open it up when Andrea came out of the office. This time I would have her. The knife would convince her. She had told me once when we were first married, that knives made her more nervous than guns. The thought of getting cut terrified her. *All the better for me.*

I stepped out of the washroom. The office lady was busy with her cigarette and stood with her back to me. She would go back in when Andrea hung up the phone. I hung around in the laundry room just outside the washrooms until the coast was clear. Just then the door to the women's washroom opened and Andrea came out. Damn! She must have gone in there while I was in the men's. She saw me and let out a shriek and ran out of the building. The office lady spun around to look. Too late to get the knife out. If Andrea had been alone it would have been different, but with the office woman there, I didn't have a chance. I made a dash for the parking lot and disappeared behind the farthest row of cars, where the land dropped off to the water.

In seconds I reached the small dock at the far corner of the parking lot and rushed down the ramp. I undid the Hawkeye's bow line, then the stern line, and tossed them aboard. I hopped on, undid the midship line and pushed the throttle forward. *Easy now! Get a grip. Wouldn't want a big cloud of black smoke giving me away. Ease that throttle forward.* Luckily I had planned ahead and had the Hawkeye facing out from the dock and left the engine idling. I'd been thinking of a quick escape with Andrea. I pounded the wheel with my fist. Once more, I was leaving without her. Pissed me off, but I wasn't giving up. I might have to take a break but once they headed north to fish, I'd find my chance.

They still didn't know I had changed the look of the boat. I'd catch them off guard one of these times. It was very solitary on the north coast with lots of anchorages tucked away behind small islets. It would be so much easier to get Andrea away from Jim when there were no other people around. I was counting on the loneliness of the north coast to work in my favour.

Chapter 38

When I came out of the washroom and stepped outside the building I looked for Joanne to ask her to keep an eye out for me. A few feet behind her, with his back to me, stood the man who had just come out of the washroom. He turned to look over his shoulder and I almost fainted with fright.

I ran towards the boatyard screaming, "Get away from me!" Joanne reached for me as I went by and I nearly knocked her over. "Call the police! I yelled into her face. I pushed her away and kept running. "Jim!" I called as loudly as I could. "Ji-i-i-m!"

Jim rushed over with the putty knife still in his hand. "What's wrong?" He looked bewildered, eyes wide. I threw myself into his arms.

"Robert!" I gulped to catch my breath, but then sobs escaped me and I could hardly speak. "He was here."

"Robert?" Jim frowned. "No. That's not possible. Not in Nanaimo."

"Yes! It was him."

"Where? In the office?"

"Outside. He came out of the washroom. Probably hiding in there."

"But you were in the office on the phone, weren't you? Is everything okay? Your parents?"

"There was no phone call. He must have made it up. Robert, I mean." I wiped my nose on my sleeve. "He was waiting for me to come out."

"Well, where is he? Are you sure it was him?"

"Jim! Dammit! It was him! Why won't you believe me?" Anger took over from fear and surged through me. "Joanne was there. She saw him. I'm not making this up. He was real."

"Let's go see Joanne, and if Robert is there ... I'll deal with him."

Jim took my hand. I pulled away and yanked back my hand. "No! I'm not going back there. He's somewhere nearby." I wasn't going to let Jim lead me right back to Robert. What if he punched him again like in the hospital? Then all he had to do was grab me and run.

"We have to get to the bottom of this. You have to come with me. I'm not leaving you alone."

I hadn't thought of that. If I was alone, he could grab me all the more easily. "Oh, Jim. What if he's still hiding behind some of the other boats in the yard?" I didn't want to go back but I was afraid to stay. I grabbed Jim's hand. "Don't let him get me."

He held my hand tightly. "Of course not!"

I thought I would faint if Robert suddenly appeared. I stayed close to Jim as we walked past the dumpster and over to the office.

Joanne came over. "I didn't call the police, Andrea. What could I say? Really. The guy didn't do anything. He just stood there and then he ran."

"What did he look like? "Which way did he go?" Jim asked.

Joanne waved her arm towards the parking lot. "Down there somewhere. He looked like he was in a pretty big hurry. He was a really good-looking guy. Tall, muscular ... a hunk."

Jim pointed and asked Joanne, "Do you know whose boat that is? The gray one just pulling out?"

"No, sorry. Not one of our customers. Never seen it before."

Jim chewed on his lower lip and his brow furrowed. He shook his finger as if he were trying to remember something, and then glanced at me. "The gray boat in French Creek. That has to be Robert's boat."

He turned to Joanne. "I think that's our man. If you notice that boat coming anywhere near here, would you mind giving us a heads up, please?"

"Sure. Will do, but what does he want?" she asked.

"He wants Andrea back. He's an abuser. So if you could help us out, we would appreciate it."

"Oh my gawd," she whispered. "Well he can't tie up there for long. It's a private dock. He'd be noticed, but if he does, I'll be sure to let you know."

Jim smiled and put an arm over my shoulders. "I'm sure everything is fine now that the gray boat is gone. Let's get back to work."

Over the next three days, we worked steadily to clean and copper paint the hull, and then paint the cap rail and the guard rail, the top of the hull, and the cabin. At night we were both exhausted and happy for a shower and bed.

We watched out for each other and I never left the boat without taking Jim with me. I asked him to stand guard by the washroom door when I went in to have a shower. Jim told me he was pretty sure that gray boat was Robert's and we knew he was gone, but I noticed that at night when we were finished work, he pulled up the ladder so no one could climb up into the boat from the parking lot.

"You know, Andrea," he said over a cup of tea, "I think when we get home, I should do the rigging at the wharf—take me a couple of days—and then we should load the boat and take off. Get away from this Robert bullshit."

"You mean, like, go fishing? This early?"

"Yeah. Well, not actually fishing yet, but leave early and make a long holiday of the trip north. We'll be safe on the boat." He watched my face for my reaction. "So what do you think?"

My smile was genuine. "I'd love to get going as soon as we can. Just you and me—one long picnic." I was only too glad to be out of Robert's reach.

"Great! You could do an inventory of what's on the boat—food and supplies—and then we could go shopping for the boat. Pick up all the non-perishable items we'll need for the summer. Then we'll get our clothes together and get going as soon as we can."

"What about the house?"

"Giselle will keep an eye on it like she always does."

I nodded. "That's so good to have friends like Giselle and Jacques. They're such fine people."

"Yeah, they sure are. I'm lucky to have them. I bring them lots of fish when I get home, but even if I didn't, they'd still look out for me."

"I can't wait to get going. On the boat we'll be like on an island fortress." *And Robert can't touch us.* "Where will we go first?"

"Over to Lund, I think. I'd like to see Stan. I owe him an explanation for why I didn't get hauled out at his boatyard this year. Don't want him to think it's anything personal."

I was bouncing on the balls of my feet. "I'll be able to see Monique." I threw my arms around Jim's neck. "Oh, thank you!" Then my smile disappeared. *What if Robert is there?*

"I know what you're thinking. And no, I don't think he'll be there. I think he'll be looking for some smaller place to hang out. A place with fewer people."

Chapter 39

Boaters were expected to travel slowly through congested harbour areas. I had the throttle up as far as I dared while inside Nanaimo's harbour. I wanted out of there. Another failure. I was heading home.

Even though I was getting tired of chasing Andrea, I simply couldn't give her up. I had to admit I had wasted a lot of time and fuel for the boat trying to get her back and every time I was left standing there, looking like a fool. Yeah, I bet it gave her a scare the other day when she found the amulet in the Serenity's wheelhouse, but what was in it for me? I didn't get to hear her shriek, or see her trembling in her boots. Too much effort and no reward for me. Waste of my time.

I thought maybe I'd get her rattled enough that I could snatch her at the shipyard in Nanaimo, but that damned office woman and her cigarette addiction fucked me up. What did she have to come outside to smoke for anyway? I was so close to snatching Andrea. I'd have had her down to the boat in a minute if I could have gotten my hands on her. A knife blade pressing on her ribs would have done the trick. Not that I would have hurt her. As long as she behaved.

I'd been sure I would get her back with that last attempt. Already imagined her in the bunk with me. We'd have motored out into the open water a little way and found a place to drop the hook. Then I'd planned to show her what she'd been missing out on—a real man to make love to her. If she had any feelings for Jim, she'd soon forget them when we made love. I could easily outdo him in that department. I slammed my hand on the wheel. Fuck! I couldn't stifle a scream of frustration. Nobody heard me out here on the water anyway. Not that I cared if they did.

Once I got that out of my system I put my head on the wheel and sobbed. *My beautiful Andrea. I have to get you back.* After that little crying jag, I felt a bit better. I looked around the Hawkeye and the empty bunk that I'd been so sure we would share that night. After my failed attempt, I lost heart. The headache came back and I had to throw the hook out as soon as I got past the islands at Departure Bay. I wanted to leave Nanaimo and my failure behind, but I badly needed to lie down. If I didn't, that headache was going to kill me.

By the time the throbbing faded, it was dawn and I made a decision to head for home—wherever that was these days—and forget, well, try to forget about Andrea. I didn't want to go back to my property with the lonely burnt down cabin. Not just yet, anyway. Someday I'd rebuild it, but I wasn't ready to face that right now—without Andrea. For now, I needed to be someplace where I wouldn't have to answer too many questions about the cabin fire, and close enough to a place where I could get groceries and a few bottles of Scotch. Yeah, quite a few bottles of Scotch. Lund was perfect. I'd grab some groceries there and then, if I felt like having more privacy, I'd go to Finn Bay just around the corner.

Two days later, I pulled in to the wharf at Lund and all the dockside spots were taken. Damned if I was going to climb over someone else's boat and all their deck clutter every time I wanted to go back and forth onto mine. Bringing bags of groceries to the boat was not easy when you had to duck under rigging and climb over ropes and other crap left lying around. Piss on this.

I was tying up in the loading zone close to the bottom of the ramp. Just got the last wrap around the bull rail of the dock when Bert showed up. Big-bellied Bert. Ha! What a specimen he was. Probably hadn't seen his own feet in twenty years.

"Can't tie up there, Robert," he said.

I pulled myself up to my full six-foot-three height and put my hands on my hips. "Says who?" *I'd show him a thing or two.*

"Didn't you just hear me say it?"

"I'll tie up wherever I want. This is a government wharf with first priority for commercial fishermen."

"Sure it is, but you still have to follow the rules." Bert pointed at my chest. "Even you!"

I spat a good gob right by his feet. "Piss on the rules. Rules are for fools."

Bert's face turned red. "You move that bloody boat right now or I'll move it for you."

"Fuck you! Think you're so important with your little wharfinger's job. Well, fuck you. This boat is staying right here."

"Fine! Then I'll just have to make that call to the RCMP and let them know you're in town. I'm sure they've been wondering where you are, after you burned down your cabin with Andrea in it." He had a smirk on his face now. "Oh yeah, Monique told me all about it. You cowardly pathetic piece of shit."

"Calling me a piece of shit?" I hauled off to punch his lights out, but just then I saw out of the corner of my eye that a few of the other boaters had gathered nearby.

No way I wanted the cops showing up and playing 20 questions with me.

"Fine! I see you have your little backup army ready. Trust me, you'd need their help if I let loose on you."

"And best you don't come back to this wharf. You're not welcome here." Bert was acting the tough guy now, with his team behind him.

"Don't know why anyone comes here anyway, the way it stinks. Why don't you clean up this pigsty?"

"That's what I'm doing right now, starting with you. Get the hell out of here and don't come back!"

"Asshole! You haven't seen the last of me."

"Well, if I do see you, it'll be too soon."

I spat again for emphasis. Got him on the shoe this time. "Ya limp prick!"

A few days later, I hit it lucky. Sarah came along as I was walking into town from Finn Bay, where I'd gone after the confrontation with Bert. Had to get my truck from behind Stan's haulout shop in Lund. Sarah pulled up in her car and gave me a ride. She'd been living alone too long, judging by the way she came onto me.

What the hell, I thought. Might as well get some action. I'd built up quite a need since Andrea took off on me. I turned on the charm and Sarah was like putty in my hands.

"Oh my GOD!" she said later. "I thought you were going to kill me with that thing." But she didn't seem afraid and the grin on her face told me she wanted more.

Chapter 40

RCMP, Powell River Detachment, Constable Jordan speaking." The voice on the other end of the line was hesitant and then gruff.

"Uh … Yeah! … I'd like to report a disturbance."

I took the caller's details. Bert Lawrence, the wharfinger at Lund, had a little run-in with one of the fishermen from the area, one Robert Bolton. He didn't want anything done just yet—only wanted to go on record as having complained, because, as he said, we hadn't heard the last of Robert Bolton.

"Say, Bill? Didn't we have a call about a Robert Bolton last fall?"

"Bolton….Yeah, that rings a bell," he said. "That's right. Lots of little incidents over the years but nothing we could ever prove."

I nodded. "This wharfinger from Lund just had a run-in with him and wanted to give us a heads up. Said Bolton always had a hot temper but it seemed like he was getting a lot more aggressive."

Bill flicked through his notebook. "Hang on, Mike. Here it is. Constable Creston from Comox Detachment called to ask if we knew anything about him. I told him what I had on file."

"Which is…?"

"He's a fisherman. Orange troller at the wharf in Lund. I had to settle a dispute there. Bit of an asshole. Very belligerent. Doesn't like to be told what to do."

Bill turned back to the computer and typed in Bolton's name. "Just a sec."

"You seem to know this guy pretty well. Any reason?"

"Here it is," he said, pointing to the screen. "Constable Andersen called from Vancouver last fall, asking a lot of questions about him. The guy burned his cabin down."

I shrugged and shook my head, not understanding. "What's the big deal about that?"

"According to the guy's wife, he set it on fire with her in it. She was found miles from nowhere, nearly dead."

"So why isn't the guy in jail?" I asked.

"'He said, she said.' Who knows what really happened? He said she was pissed off with him and she was the one who burned it down. We'll never know what really happened. Crown Prosecutor didn't want to hear it. Never make a case, he said."

"Well, there's no point in getting all fired up over a 'he said, she said' thing. You'd never win. And anyway, in the end, the wife always caves and wants to take back everything she said in a complaint."

"I'm not so sure this one will cave. She went to desperate measures to get away from the guy, according to Constable Andersen. She'd walked the coastline for miles trying to get to Hope Bay and escape Bolton. Apparently he kept her in the cabin and abused her."

I couldn't stomach guys like that, taking out their insecurities on women. "That sonofabitch."

"Here's another incident I noted down. Squirrel Cove. Air ambulance was called out and I had to attend because there was a scuffle. They said Bolton had been mouthing off at some guys at the wharf, and they'd finally had enough and laid a beating on him. The guys involved said he fell down the ramp and broke his leg. I think he might have had some help getting down the ramp, but Bolton was such a loudmouth and so belligerent, even with his broken leg, that I thought he might have gotten just what he asked for."

"Sounds like a bit of a character."

Bill leaned back in his chair to allow me to look at the monitor. "Oh, and look at this. Our boy's been around. Minor complaints going back years. Mostly fights. Scrapping with bystanders. Shot some guy's dog. Bastard. Oh wait! That was less than two years ago."

"Where's he from? Family? Where's he living?"

"Born Bakersfield, California. Landed immigrant status. Parents deceased. Brother in an institution in Bakersfield.

"According to Constable Andersen he's presumed to be living on his boat since he burned his cabin down."

I poured myself another cup of Bill's foul-tasting coffee and listened as he read on, going back even farther. "Minor scrapes with the law. Usually fighting. Domestic abuse charges filed by a former girlfriend, Linda Sampson, but charges were dropped. Lack of evidence and she wouldn't testify. A string of other women complaining of physical excesses, but not wanting to press charges."

"This him?" I pointed at the screen. "Jeezus! I thought it was going to be some ugly mug with all that history, but he's a really good-looking guy. I can see why a girl would hook up with him. But then look out if his temper acts up."

"And here's a report from Comox," Bill said. "Tried to kidnap his estranged wife by drugging her with Rohypnol. This guy sounds like trouble. Maybe we should take a drive and pay him a visit."

"Yeah, sure. Soon as I get my reports written. Doesn't sound urgent but we should probably check into it in a day or two. I have a feeling we haven't heard the last of this guy. He shows all the signs of escalating. Probably wouldn't hurt to pay him a visit and remind him to behave."

Chapter 41

At the top of the wharf, Jim handed the house keys over to Giselle and Jacques. "Thanks for the ride," he said. "I'll check in every couple of days with the satellite phone. You've got the number?"

"Yes, yes, of course." Giselle patted her shoulder bag. "I've got it right here in my wallet."

Jacques gave me a hug and then shook Jim's hand while I hugged Giselle. "You two stick together and you'll be fine," he said. "Don't worry about the house. We'll look after everything."

"Thanks, you guys," Jim said. "We'll be in touch. Take care of yourselves while we're gone."

Aboard the Serenity, Jim started the engine. She looked beautiful, all spruced up with fresh paint and scrubbed clean. After a few minutes, when Jim gave me the nod, I untied the lines and the boat drifted away from the dock.

That small movement, as we floated away from the security and responsibilities of land, had an odd effect on us both. "We're off," Jim said with a huge smile. "Don't you feel like a huge weight has been lifted off our shoulders?"

I nodded. "It's like leaving all your troubles behind." I glanced up at Jim and added quickly, "Not that I didn't like being at the house, but I mean—" *But would I measure up when we were on the boat? What if I had to do something like drive the boat if Jim felt sick, or what if we hit really bad weather and I couldn't handle it?*

"I know what you mean." He pulled me in for a warm hug. "Mmm ... this is nice."

I pushed him away gently. "Later. Let's get out of the harbour first."

As we rounded the point of land that protected Comox, the motion of the boat changed to a slight pitching up and down. The waves slapped at the hull. "Going to be a bit breezy till the tide changes," Jim said. "But then we should be fine for crossing over to Lund."

I grinned. "I can hardly wait to see Monique again. She should be finished work by the time we get there. Said she'd be watching for us."

"I don't know if I should be jealous of Monique or not." Jim's crooked smile told me he wasn't sure of anything where Monique was concerned.

"Don't worry. She's got Max. Er ... Maxine. She was at Giselle's party. Remember her? Back when Monique and I came over to Comox that time after we first met you. When Monique told me she had Max, I thought she'd gone straight. She laughed and said, 'Maxine.'"

"That rings a bell, but I also remember that Monique was pretty serious about wanting you rather than Max." He pulled me closer to him as I stood beside the captain's bench by the wheel.

"Monique loves me—in her way—no doubt about it, but she's very understanding. She would never do anything to hurt either of us." I kissed Jim on the cheek. "And neither would I."

We lapsed into silence then, each of us reminiscing about our days in Lund. "I wonder if Sarah is still in Lund," I said "There's one I wouldn't trust."

"Sarah? Why not?"

"I think she still carries a torch for you. Before she knew that we had anything going on, she told me about deckhanding with this handsome guy and how the sex was so good—"

"She said that?" Jim grinned. "She liked it then?"

I pinched Jim's arm. "She did, but she pretended it didn't matter that it didn't work out."

"So what's not to trust about that?"

"Well, two minutes after she told me all that, she started in again, all wispy, dreamy, thinking she could have you back." I thought about those days when I had worked part time in Sarah's gift shop in Lund. "She's going to be really pissed when she sees us together. I don't think she knows."

When we pulled in to Lund, Bert came puffing down to greet us. Jim had just pulled in to his favourite spot. Luckily there was a dockside space available, so we wouldn't have to tie next to another boat and climb all over it every time we got on or off the boat.

"See you're right in your old spot there, Jim," Bert said. He took the stern line and tied it while Jim took care of the bow. I had already tied the midship line as we came alongside the dock.

"Yeah, I figured you must have been saving it for me." Jim grinned and shook Bert's hand. "Nice to see you, Bert. How've you been?"

"Oh, not too bad. Kind of early this year, aren't you?" He turned to me, smiled, and said, "And how's the best wharfinger's helper I ever had?"

"Fine," I said. "Just fine."

"Sure is good to see you two together," he said.

I looked at my feet and then cleared my throat. "You know, Bert, you were right about Robert. But things turned out all right after all now that I'm with Jim."

"I figured it was meant to be after he fished you out of the water on your first day of work here. You remember that?"

My face felt warmer than it was a few seconds ago. "How could I forget something like that?" Bert turned to talk to Jim. "So you're not here to work on the boat. She's all spiffied up already. How come you're over this way so early?"

"We just thought we'd like to get away and have a bit of a holiday before the fishing starts." Jim leaned closer to Bert and lowered his voice, "And anyway, Robert has been ... well ... kind of stalking Andrea, so we wanted to get away from him."

Bert's eyes grew big and round. "Crikey! Did you come to the wrong place!"

My hands flew to my chest. "Why? What's wrong?" I asked.

"He's over at Finn Bay, I hear. See him around the gift shop sometimes, talking to Sarah. Boat looks different too. Took off the bow poles. Put on a dodger. Painted it gray. Painted right over the name of the boat." Bert took a breath and hooked his thumbs in his belt loops. "Yup! He's a strange one. It's almost like he's trying to hide the boat."

Oh shit! I was afraid of this.

"All gray, eh? Dodger, you say?" Jim nodded slowly. "That explains a lot," he said under his breath.

"You're safe here," Bert said. "I told him not to come around here anymore. Had a bit of a run-in with him, and he's not welcome at this wharf anymore, so don't worry. Any problems, you just give me a holler." He turned to go back up to the office and raised an arm into the air. "Nice to see you both."

Chapter 42

O h, Jim!" I grabbed his arm and hoped he wouldn't notice my trembling. "Let's not stay."

He looked at me with his face screwed up in disbelief. "But we just got here!"

"I know, but I didn't think Robert was going to be here. And what's he visiting Sarah for?"

Jim gave me a questioning look. "What do you care? Jealous?"

"No, of course not. But I just don't get it. Why would he be moving in on her?"

"Maybe it's her moving in on him. Robert's a handsome guy—if you can see past his personality disorder—and Sarah is man-hungry." Jim shrugged. "Makes sense to me."

A shiver ran over me. "She's in for an ugly surprise."

Jim put his hands on my shoulders and looked into my eyes. "Look, I know it makes you nervous hearing all about Robert being nearby. We won't stay long, but I really should go have a quick visit with Stan. I've been going to his haulout facility every year until now. This is the first time I've gone someplace else. He's been good to me, so I can't leave without saying hello. I'll just run over to see him for a few minutes. I won't be long. If you want, we can leave in the morning."

Oh, I wanted to run. My stomach was about to drop on the floor and I thought I'd pass out from fright, but

I had to pull myself together and make it look as if everything was under control.

"Okay. That sounds good." I looked past Jim's shoulders at someone waving madly at the top of the ramp. "Oh my God, it's Monique!"

She was as cute as ever in a boyish way. She ran down the dock and hugged me hard. "Andrea! So good to see you!" Monique turned to Jim and gave him a quick hug. "Nice to see you too. Good trip over?"

"Yeah, not bad at all. How've you been?"

"Oh well, you know. Working all de time." Monique turned back to me. "So can you both come over for supper tonight? It will be simple. Maybe 'amburgers on de barbecue?"

"Sounds good. We can catch up on what's happening," I said. "What time?"

"Come over any time." Monique gave me another hug and a kiss on the cheek. "It's so good to see you."

"Okay, how about if I come with you while Jim goes to visit Stan, and then he can join us when he's done?" I turned to Jim as I spoke, nodding my head, looking for agreement.

"Perfect," said Jim and Monique at the same time.

Monique and I walked up the ramp and along the road to her rental. "Still in the same place?" I asked.

"For sure t'ing," Monique said. "Why move when you don't 'ave to? It's a good place, and Max ... Maxine ... likes it."

"So how is it with you two?" I couldn't help but ask. "Do you love her?" I half hoped that Monique would say no, but I immediately chided myself for being so uncharitable.

"Oh, of course I do ... but you know, Andrea," and she lowered her voice, "I would drop her in a minute if you would come back to me." She squeezed my hand. I thought about pulling away, but I loved Monique in my own way, and it felt good to be here with her.

"Well, Max is lucky I'm not gay, because I would choose you if I were." And it was true, but the "if" was a big "IF," and it would never happen. I had let Monique lead me astray somewhat when I first met her, but in the end, I had to confront my feelings and admit that no matter how much I liked Monique, I was not gay and we would never make it as a couple. Sexually, I liked men a lot more than women.

We slowed as we came up to Sarah's gift shop. "Still a funky little place, isn't it?" I said. "It was kind of nice working there, meeting lots of people, and seeing all that beautiful artwork."

"Yeah, she does 'ave nice t'ings."

Just then, Sarah came out of the shop door to take in her sandwich board and close up for the day. "Hi, Monique!" she called to her.

I raised my hand to wave. "Hi, Sarah."

Sarah dropped the sandwich board. "Andrea?" She clapped a hand over her mouth. "What are *you* doing here?" She smiled as if she was glad to see me, but it looked forced, almost like a thinly disguised snarl.

"Just visiting on our way north."

"You and ... Jim, I guess?" Her eyes narrowed ever so slightly, but a fake smile remained pasted onto her face.

"That's right." I squirmed inwardly. "I guess you heard that Robert and I have split."

She waggled her head back and forth. "Hmpf! I heard that Jim stole Robert's wife."

"It wasn't quite like that," I said, "and anyway, where are you getting this information?"

"Well, if you must know, Robert told me." She stuck out her chin and raised her nose, looking down at me under half-closed eyelids. "He's been staying here sometimes." I thought she would piss herself with all that gloating.

"You're going to 'ave trouble, Sarah," Monique said. "Dat man is not right up dere." She tapped the side of her head a few times.

"You just don't understand him," Sarah said.

"Hah! And you do?!" I said. "You're headed for trouble, girl." *And maybe you deserve it.*

Monique put a hand on my arm to calm me. "Do you know where Robert is now?" I asked.

"Of course. He's over at Finn Bay. That's where he keeps the boat."

My nerves jangled at the thought of him so close by. "Well, do us both a favour, would you, Sarah, if he comes by, don't tell him I'm here. He'll most likely see the boat anyway, but I don't want any trouble."

"I'll tell him or not, depends if I feel like it or not. You stole Jim away from me, so I'm not going to make it easy for you to steal Robert back too." She snorted. "And here I thought you were my friend when I confided in you about Jim. You did me a dirty. I don't owe you anything."

"Jim and I had nothing going on back then. If he came to help me get away from Robert, he did it because he wanted to, not because I asked."

Sarah let out a big sigh. "Well, it doesn't matter anymore. Water under the bridge. I've got Robert now. He's quite the lover, and handsome too. You're going to be sorry you ran off."

I shook my head slowly. "You're the one who's going to be sorry." It was hard to believe Sarah was so naive. But then, hadn't I been the same, or worse, when I let Robert sweep me off my feet like that?

"Are you threatening me? You'll be sorry talking to me like that. Just wait till Robert finds out you've been threatening me and badmouthing him."

"No. I'm not threatening you at all. Be careful, Sarah. Robert isn't who or what you think he is." Tears welled in my eyes, but they were not tears of regret or love.

Monique pulled at my sleeve. "Come on, Andrea."

"Be careful, Sarah," I said over my shoulder.

Monique hooked her arm under mine and hustled me along the road towards her place. Maxine was waiting in the doorway. She stepped out to greet me. "Hey, Andrea. How are you?" She hugged me hard and I caught a whiff of manly aftershave. She was a big woman, quite muscular. Her strawberry blonde hair was cut very short around her ears and neck, while longer tresses with a bold purple streak covered the top in a way that was manly, yet fashionable. Large silver hoops dangled from her ears.

"What happened?" Maxine asked. "You both look shaken up and white as ghosts."

Monique waved her concern away. "Oh, nothing. Just dat Sarah. She's all in a flap over Robert."

"Well, she needn't worry about me wanting him back," I said.

"We're going to 'ave a barbecue and not worry about it." Monique gave us a firm nod as if to punctuate her decision.

Just then we turned at the sound of tires spinning on the gravel road. I recognized Sarah's car—the one Sarah, Monique, and I had carpooled in several times to do our shopping in Powell River. Monique would get our groceries and I would help Sarah shop for Dollar Store items to resell in her gift shop. She was sneaky, how she mixed in the cheap items among the finer artwork. Seemed she was still sneaky now. "I bet she's heading for Finn Bay."

"We'll soon know, if she turns left at the top of the road," Maxine said.

We craned our necks watching the brake lights of her car come on as she approached the intersection. "Shit! She *is* going out there," I said. "She's going to tell Robert." My throat closed up and I gulped down a knot of fear. "I have to go to Stan's to find Jim. Monique, I'm sorry. I don't think we can stay after all. Robert has been really aggressive. I can't stay here if he's nearby." I gave Monique a hug while she stood with her mouth partly open.

Maxine came forward and squeezed my hand. "You do what you have to do. We'll walk over to Stan's with you just to make sure you find Jim. Won't we, Monique?"

"Oh, for sure t'ing! Let's go before dat bitch brings Robert back here." Monique's teeth were clenched and her cheeks were tightened into two hard lumps. "Stupid, stupid bitch!"

We found Jim and Stan talking in the shop behind the haulout area. The girls helped me explain what had happened, and Jim agreed that we would be better off away from the wharf if Robert came down there.

We said our goodbyes and promised to reconnect one day, maybe in Comox instead of in Lund. Monique and I had tears in our eyes, but Maxine smiled happily and wished us a good trip.

I was so relieved when we pulled away from the wharf. "I'm sorry, Jim. I—"

"Don't worry about it." He wrapped me up in his arms and I felt safe again.

"I was thinking we could go just across the way to the Copeland Islands. There's a little bay we can anchor in. It's easy to get in and out of," I said.

"I know the one," Jim said. "Good idea. Then tomorrow, we'll get a really early start and be gone from here and free of Robert's shadow."

"That's good," I said. "Yes, that will be really good. And it's still early enough that we can do our own barbecue on the back deck tonight."

"I packed a bottle of wine that will be perfect for this special occasion."

"Occasion?" I asked.

"It's two years ago today that I met you. You remember? That was the day you fell off the dock."

"Oh gawd!" I moaned. "Do you have to keep bringing that up?"

"If you hadn't fallen into the water, I wouldn't have been able to come to the rescue with dry clothes, and we might not be here together right now."

"If I had known it would bring us together, I would have jumped in voluntarily, but maybe I would have picked a less grimy part of the dock. I looked a fright!"

"Ah, but that was all part of the fun."

"For you!"

"It was, in a way," he said with a smirk, "but you clean up very nicely."

Jim checked the monitor and tapped the spot where we would turn into the bay on the south end of the Copelands. "That's a good spot."

"I know it well. It's where Robert took me for a picnic when we first met."

"Yes, you mentioned that...."

"I should have picked up on some of the signals way back then that he had a few screws loose."

"He still does." Jim snorted. "What a piece of work he is." He glanced over at me. "Hey! Don't worry. We're away from Lund and Finn Bay. He doesn't know where we've gone, and even if he knows, you're safe with me. And we're both safe on the boat. He can't do anything to you. I won't let him. I promise."

I wanted to believe Jim, but I couldn't help looking back through the wheelhouse door to check for other boat traffic. So far, there was only the empty expanse of water bordered by rocky hills on either side of the passage. So far....

Chapter 43

I was tied to the floats at Finn Bay. The slight rocking of the boat told me that someone had just stepped aboard the Hawkeye. I put my book down and sat up in the bunk.

Sarah stood in the doorway with a funny look on her face.

"What's up?" I asked.

She stepped over the sill of the wheelhouse door. "Hi Robert. Just wondering if you felt like having company tonight."

"Oh." I put a marker in my book and stood up. This was going to be more interesting than what I was reading. "Make yourself at home." I pulled her close and kissed her. Hard.

She pushed me away. "Robert!" She wiped her mouth with the back of her hand. "Not so hard."

I gave her nose a peck. "Sorry, but you see what you do to me."

She smiled. So predictable. Too easy. But what the hell. She fucked like a mink. I pulled her sweater over her head.

"At least close the door," she said.

When I turned back from closing and latching the door she was already stepping out of her jeans. She was taller than Andrea and a bit of a bone rack, but she had the parts that mattered. I pushed my hand into her panties and her legs opened willingly while her hands fumbled with my zipper. Sarah writhed a little dance as she tugged my jeans downward. I helped her by stepping out of them.

Once I was clear of the hobbling pant legs, I pushed her onto the bunk and yanked the panties off her. They tore as my fingers went through the flimsy material.

"Uh—Robert! Stop!" She tried to sit up but I pushed her back down.

"I'll buy you a new pair," and I was in her, pumping hard until she whimpered and pleaded for me to stop. I came then and rolled off her. "Okay. I'll stop."

She lay there with tears on her red cheeks, the mascara smeared under her eyes giving her the look of an unhappy raccoon.

"What's the matter?" I asked her. "Isn't that what you wanted?"

"Y-yes ... no...." She sniffed and wiped her nose on her arm.

"Well, which is it—yes or no?"

Sarah sat up and grabbed some paper towel off the table beside the bunk. She pressed a bunch of it between her legs. "Yes, but you hurt me." She turned a shoulder toward me and looked away.

I stroked her hair and kissed her forehead. "Aw ... I'm sorry. You know I wouldn't hurt you on purpose."

She picked up her shredded panties and held them up. Then a little laugh escaped her. "You owe me a pair of panties."

"Said I'd buy you new ones, didn't I? Next time I'm in town."

We pulled our clothes back on.

Had to appease her and keep her happy and putting out for me. "I was going to come over to Lund and see if you wanted to go for a burger with me."

Sarah pulled a hairbrush out of her bag and struggled with the knots in her hair. "Could do."

I took the brush from her. "Here. Let me do that."

She turned her back so I could brush her hair. The strands were thin and blonde, but limp. I couldn't help thinking of Andrea's thick wavy brown hair. "Looks like you got a few tangles rolling around in my bed." I pulled the brush harder.

"Ow! Oh, Robert. Wait. Here I'll do it."

"So how about that burger? I don't feel much like cooking on the boat tonight, but I seem to have worked up an appetite."

"You want to come with me in my car?"

"No, I think I'll take my truck. Then you don't have to drive me home."

"Or you could stay over at my place," she said.

I let that suggestion hang. I could make up my mind later on. Nice to have the choice. On the drive over to Lund I felt pretty good. I'd just taken care of my needs and if I played my cards right, I could probably get them taken care of again after supper. Or at the very least, in the morning.

At the hotel I parked the truck next to Sarah's car. We were about to go into the hotel restaurant when I looked out at the harbour. The sky was getting darker but I could still make out the shape of a boat that had just left the dock. It sure looked familiar.

"You know," I said to Sarah, "that boat sure looks a lot like the Serenity."

"Hmm...." Sarah tugged on my sleeve. "Come on. Let's get a table before the place fills up."

Chapter 44

It was a gorgeous day and I didn't feel like sitting behind a desk answering the phone.

"Bill, what do you say we take a ride out to Lund this morning and look up our friend, Bolton?"

"Sure. Sounds like a plan. You driving, Mike?"

"Yep. I think I can find my way to Lund. Big 17-mile trip. Be good to get out of the office."

"There's a great little bakeshop at the wharf head. We have to go to the wharf to see this Bert anyway, right, and get his story, so we just might have to stop for one of those cinnamon rolls they're famous for."

Bill grabbed his jacket and cap. "What're we waitin' for?"

I was glad it was a slow day. I didn't mind a change of pace after the rash of break-ins we'd had to deal with last week.

I parked at the top of the wharf, by the office. I got out slowly, to look all the more officious, fixed my cap and stepped into the office. A huge pot-bellied man came up to the counter to speak to me.

"I'm looking for Bert Lawrence?"

The man's fingers drummed on the counter. "That's me. What can I do for you?"

"I'm Constable Jordan. I spoke with you on the phone."

Bert's eyes lit up. "Oh yeah! Right!" He stuck out his hand. "Pleased to meet you."

I nodded. "Have you had any more trouble with Robert Bolton? Seen him around?"

"He hasn't been back with his boat since I told him he wasn't welcome here, but I've seen him around town with his truck. He's spending time at Sarah's gift shop across the street there." He pointed at a house with a covered veranda. "All's been quiet here. Just a matter of time, though."

"Until what?"

"Until he blows up again. He's like a powder keg waiting for a match to drop."

"Really! Have you had other incidents before the one when you told him he wasn't welcome here?"

Bert shook his head and huffed in disgust. "Oh Christ, yes! Seems like every time his boat was here there was some kind of trouble. Doesn't even have to be a real problem. Somebody might have just looked at him the wrong way, and it goes from there."

"How long has that been going on?" I asked.

"He was always an odd one, and not overly friendly, but seems like since his wife ran away from him last fall, he's been blowing up at the slightest thing."

"Do you know where we can find him? We'd like to have a little chat with him."

Bert flipped his hand to indicate the gift shop up the street. "Try Sarah's. He's been there quite a bit."

I touched my cap. "Thanks, Bert."

Up the street at the gift shop, we knocked and entered. Bill let out a low whistle. "Nice stuff!

I turned over a price tag. "Outta your range, unless you plan on doing a lot of overtime."

"Can I help you?"

Bill was quick to take the lead on this one. "Are you Sarah?" He liked skinny blondes. I let him ask the questions.

"When was the last time you saw Robert Bolton?" he asked.

"Last night," she said without hesitation.

"Is he living here?"

"No, he stays on his boat most of the time."

"But Bert said Robert's boat isn't welcome here."

Sarah inhaled deeply and let the air out slowly. "Yes, well, Bert doesn't understand Robert."

"You haven't had any problems with Robert?"

"No, I haven't. He's really sweet," she said. "Has that bitch been saying things about him?"

"Who might that be, ma'am?"

"Andrea. His ex. She was here a few days ago. She's got a nerve coming around to taunt him like that."

"Like what, ma'am?"

"Well, she had to know he would know she was here when she came in with her boyfriend on the Serenity." Her eyes went narrow and her mouth muscles worked even though she had stopped talking.

"Is Andrea here now?" Bill asked.

"She's gone. She didn't stay long when she heard that Robert is mine now."

"Do you know where we might find Andrea?" I asked.

"She and Jim are heading north to go commercial fishing. You won't find them unless you have a boat."

"Do you know where we can find Robert?"

"Probably buried in a ton of boat work over in Finn Bay."

"In the yard? Or at the wharf?"

"Right now he should be tied to the dock there."

We took our leave of Sarah and headed out to Finn Bay. "Wow!" I said. "Did you detect some bitterness there about Andrea being around? Maybe she felt threatened?"

"No kidding. I don't think Andrea wanted Robert back after running away from him. Sounds like she's got a new boyfriend now."

I looked at Bill. "Well, let's hear what Robert has to say."

Finn Bay was very small. Just the dock and a few buildings. We asked the first person we saw which boat was the Hawkeye.

"She's gone. Left this morning. Just as well. The asshole."

"I guess that takes care of that," I said to Bill. "I think it's time to go back and grab a coffee and a couple of those famous cinnamon rolls."

Chapter 45

Early May could be a bit rainy, but this year the sun was out more often than not and the coast was warm and steamy during the daytime.

Once we got away from "Robert-tainted" places like Lund and the Copelands, Andrea was much calmer and more relaxed.

"Just wait till you see this place," I told her. I turned the boat to starboard to follow the coastline. "The Copelands are pretty, but you'll love Tenedos Bay and Unwin Lake beyond it."

"Can we go ashore in the skiff?" Andrea asked. "I'd love to explore a bit. Most of the coast is so steep and rocky and you can't really go for much of a walk. I miss being able to walk anywhere when we're on the boat for so long."

"I know what you mean. There's a trail at the head of the bay, so we'll throw out the hook and check it out."

About twenty minutes later it was time to find a good spot. "Want to go up front and kick the anchor over? We're almost there."

"Sure thing." She jumped up to go around the outside of the wheelhouse to the bow.

"Wait for my signal," I added in case she thought I meant to do it right away. That would have been something, running over my own anchor line.

"Of course!" She rolled her eyes at me. Hadn't meant to insult her, but these days with more and more women doing men's work, you couldn't be too careful. I'd learned never to assume they knew what they were doing.

I did a circle of the bay to be sure of the bottom before dropping the hook. I had seen a sailboater do a dumb thing in this bay one summer. The skipper had thrown out the anchor and gone to have a nap. In a few hours the tide had gone out and the back end of the sailboat was high and dry on a hummock that he hadn't known was there. Luckily he hadn't tipped over too far and the tide came back in shortly after that, floating him up again.

"Okay!" I hollered. "Kick her out!" Once the length of chain had gone over the side after the anchor, the heavy anchor line followed for several more fathoms. I liked to have lots of scope in case the breeze came up and we turned. Didn't want to drag anchor.

I shut the engine down and punched in the knob for the oil alarm when the pressure dropped and the bell rang. I always liked to wait for it to ring. That way I knew it was still working properly. If the pressure ever dropped while I was running, I could trust the alarm to ring and warn me.

"Sure is quiet when the engine's stopped," Andrea said. "So nice." She let out a big sigh and smiled. "This is a beautiful place. Can't wait to go ashore."

"Let's lower the skiff over the side and then we can grab some things," I said.

"What kinds of 'things'?" she asked.

"The little Ziploc of survival gear, water bottles, and bring a windbreaker even though it seems hot. Put on long pants, and we'll throw together a quick snack."

"Why long pants?"

"Deer flies. Mosquitoes. Branches. You'll see. Maybe bring the fly dope."

I pulled the skiff up well out of reach of the tide that would come in while we were ashore and tied the painter to a heavy rock far up past the high tide mark. We gathered our packs and headed for the trail.

Andrea was already up on the grassy area where a parks sign with a map told us, "You are here."

"Read this, Jim!" she called. "They've had a nuisance black bear in the area. Should we maybe not go up that trail?"

I grinned at her and pulled a can of pepper spray out of my pack. "Never leave home without it."

"I didn't know you had that," she said. "I used to have a can of bear spray for mushroom picking. I mean I had it with me in my pack when I fled from Robert, but when I got to the hospital, all that was gone."

"We should probably get you a new one. You never know when it might come in handy." I didn't expect to ever have to use it, but I always had it on hand for going ashore. Either that or my rifle, and in this case, it made sense to throw the can in the pack. "But that sign was here last year too, so don't worry. I guess the bears get too used to people coming and going all the time and they come by so frequently that the Parks people don't even bother changing the sign." I pointed up the trail. "Shall we?"

The trail went uphill away from the beach. Huge fir tree roots had groped their way across the path occasionally gripping large rocks embedded there. I kept my eyes on the trail, going around puddles here and there and stepping off into the woods for one twenty-foot section of pure mud. After that, the path was dryer and smoother. In a few moments I caught a glimpse of Unwin Lake.

A bird shrieked repeatedly. It continued and grew louder as we neared the lake.

"What is that noise?" Andrea searched the trees looking for the source of the sound.

"Up there." I pointed. "In the snag. See the hole? Watch it."

We stood still but the shrieking continued. "I see it! I see it!" Andrea said. "It's a woodpecker of some kind, isn't it?"

"Yeah, I think it's a Downy. That chick is just about ready to leave the nest."

"What a fuss it's making."

"Wants to be fed. Stand still and be quiet as you can."

In a few moments, the parent bird flew up to the hole in the snag, the chick stuck his head and chest out and opened his beak wide. "Some poor bug just got eaten."

Andrea batted at a deer fly. "That's good. I hope some of these pests get eaten too." She slapped her shoulder. "Ouch! Oh crikey, they bite!"

"Keep moving. They're the worst when you stand still. I know I just told you to stand still, but maybe that wasn't a good idea." I waved at a deer fly buzzing around Andrea's head. "You go ahead. I'm just going to take a quick photo of the woodpeckers and I'll be right behind you." Moving towards the lower edge of the lake, Andrea ran along the path slapping at her upper arms as she went.

"Here's a place we can get out on these huge rocks," she called. "Maybe the flies won't be as bad out there." She stepped out onto a rock that was half the size of my boat and stood there with her arms stretched out wide. "Isn't this beautiful?" she said. "Jim?" She spun around. "Where are you?"

"I'm coming. Don't sit down. Stand tall, Andrea." I fumbled in my pack for the bear spray and stumbled along the path towards her. Just beyond the big rock, on one of the smaller boulders I had spotted the head of a black bear.

"Wh-what?" she said in a quavery voice.

"Stand up tall. Raise your arms up. I'm coming with the bear spray."

The bear briefly stood on his hind legs, and turned to scamper away on the trail. I reached Andrea who lowered her arms as her knees buckled. "Oh my God, Jim. Oh my God! In all the time I was traveling through the bush and trying to escape Robert, I never saw a bear and here we are just ten minutes from the skiff and ... oh my God." She hugged me tightly and even as she hugged me she twisted her neck to look up the trail for the bear.

"Well, what do you want to do?" I asked. "Do you want to stay and have a picnic here?"

"Are you crazy?" she yelled. Then she saw my grin.

"Actually, we'd better get the hell out of here, especially with our picnic in our backpacks. You go first and I'll be right behind you. If the bear turns around and decides to try to catch up to us, I'll have the bear spray handy."

Andrea didn't waste any time moving along the path. "Don't run," I told her. "Just walk fast."

"No problem. You just try to keep up with me."

As she went past the snag with the shrieking woodpecker chick, she said, "Maybe that's what he was shrieking about."

"Naw, I don't think so. That's pretty standard baby talk for Downies." I looked over my shoulder, saw nothing, and hustled to keep up to Andrea.

Back at the beach Andrea already had the skiff untied and her pack thrown into it. I put my pack in and pushed the skiff out into the water.

"Okay, hop in at the bow and I'll tow us out a bit so I can start the motor." I stuffed my pantlegs into my rubber boots and waded out beside the skiff.

Andrea grabbed an oar and pushed it into the rocky bottom to keep the boat from drifting into shallow water again while I got in and pulled the cord to start the motor.

"You've done this before," I said.

She nodded. "Lots of times."

We putted out a little way and turned to look back at our aborted picnic venture. A black shaggy figure sauntered down to the beach and casually sniffed the air in our direction. Then he turned his back on us and began turning over rocks on the beach in search of crabs.

Chapter 46

Since the black bear cut short our picnic on the beach, we ate our sandwiches on the boat and decided to enjoy the last rays of sunshine on the deck. Jim set up a folding lawn chair for me beside the hatch cover. I slouched to lie back in the chair and catch the warmth of the sun on my face. To heck with the wrinkles I was inviting. I'd worry about that tomorrow.

Jim appeared by my side with a bowl of sweet green grapes that he had just washed. He picked one of them and held it in front of my mouth.

I smiled. "You mean you're not going to peel it for me?"

"Don't push your luck," he growled. He disappeared into the wheelhouse and came back on deck a few minutes later carrying two wine glasses and an open wine bottle with a dish towel wrapped around it.

"Oh...." I moaned. "I could get used to this."

"I thought it would be nice to drink to our freedom."

"Freedom from...?"

"Freedom from Robert's harassment." Jim sat on the hatch cover and beamed at me happily.

We clinked glasses with extra gusto on that toast. "This is one of the most precious moments ever." I felt tears welling.

"I love you," we said together.

We chatted our way easily through another glass of wine and then Jim said he'd like to tie a bit of gear, to have it ready for fishing in a couple of weeks. He sat at the helm where he had fixed an eyebolt solidly into the wood. He could put the hook of the spoon through this eyebolt and pull tightly as he fastened the fishing line on the other end of the lure with a sturdy knot. It was easy work but time consuming.

While Jim tied gear, I lay back in the lawn chair, resting my neck on the back support, legs sprawled out in front of me, soaking up the sun. "Mmm ... I love this," I murmured. If only my life could be like this forever. I was in heaven. Things were going to work out just fine.

Our next day's travel was a confirmation of that feeling I'd had, that my life was on track at last. We got up early and retraced our path past the Mink Islands that stand guard on Tenedos Bay, and then veered to starboard through Desolation Sound. A hint of a dark cloud came over me as we passed Robert's property where I had narrowly escaped when he burned down the cabin.

"I see it's still not rebuilt," Jim said. "Can't blame him, really. Why would he want to rebuild it if he doesn't have you?"

I clung to Jim's arm and shivered until we passed the charred remains. "No boat tied to the dock," I said. "At least that's one good thing. He must be staying back in Lund with Sarah now."

We rounded a point and I was amazed at the huge body of water that stretched out on the starboard side of the boat. "Wow! Are we going all the way to the end of this bay?"

"Arm, and no," Jim said.

"Something wrong with your arm?" I asked.

Jim shook his head. "Arm. It's called an arm, not a bay. It's really long, like an arm."

"Where are we going then?" I had to admit it was beautiful but other than a place to spend the night, I wasn't sure why we had turned in here.

"This is a Provincial Marine Park. There's a lake a little way in, and it should be clear of bears. But the best part is a surprise."

We were still quite some distance from the anchorage when I saw the huge waterfall. "Is that it?" I asked. "Beautiful!"

"But just wait," Jim said.

We anchored in the small bay near the waterfall and lowered the skiff into the water. There wasn't a soul around and no sound except for the rushing of the waterfall and the odd eagle cry. The clunk of the skiff on the side of the Serenity's hull seemed like a rude intrusion.

"What a perfect anchorage." I couldn't believe any place could be so beautiful. The sunny day helped, of course, but everything around us was pure and natural.

We packed the usual basics, just as we had at Unwin Lake. Jim threw an extra bag into the skiff, and we went ashore.

"What's in the bag?" I asked.

"Secret." He smirked. "Don't touch."

I shrugged and tried to pretend I didn't care. Jim's smile played around his lips every time he saw me eyeing the bag.

The hike along the trail to Cassel Lake got our blood pumping. My leg muscles were happy to have a workout after being cooped up in the boat for 24 hours.

Where the trail reached the lake, I stood on a monstrous slope of rock. "What a huge lake!" The hillside seemed to slide into the water.

"Be careful there," Jim said. "It's a bit of a drop off at the end of the rock."

"I'm OK. I have good rubber on these runners." Still, I thought it might be wise to clamber back up towards the trail. "Should we sit here and have our lunch?"

Jim was already taking out our sandwiches and water bottles. He took off his jacket and spread it out on the rocky slope. "Sir Walter Raleigh, at your service, Ma'am."

I gave Jim a kiss and hugged him before sitting down on his jacket. "I can't believe how lucky I am." I thought of all the times I had been with Robert out in the woods near our cabin and never once did I feel the urge to kiss or hug him. I'd learned to be too afraid to initiate anything like that with him. So many times what started out good with him had ended with me getting hurt. After a while, I hated him so much that being close to him was the last thing in the world I wanted. But with Jim, all my dreams were coming true.

When we returned to the skiff, Jim took us away from shore and steered towards the waterfall. Near it, he found a place to bring the skiff ashore again and he picked up the black plastic bag he had stashed in the bow of the skiff.

"Let's go," he said.

"Where are we going?"

"You'll see. Just follow me."

He picked his way towards the waterfall. I followed behind him. Closer to the falls, he said, "The spray is making our clothes damp. Better take them off." He still had that funny smirk on his face.

"Are you serious?" I asked, but he was already taking his shirt off.

"Yup! Come on. Off with the clothes. All of them."

"All of them? What if—"

"What if someone sees us?" He had his pants off by that time. "Woohoo!" he yelled. "Come on, Andrea. Off with the clothes. There's no one here." His voice echoed across the water to bounce off the hills beyond.

The sun was shining on Jim's gorgeous body. He still had a bit of his Hawaiian tan left except on his white buns. I glanced around one last time and took off my T-shirt and pants.

"Panties too." He reached over to pull them down and nuzzled my shivering nipples as he lowered my last piece of clothing to the ground. When he stood up and pulled me close to him, his hardness left no doubt about what would happen next. Jim took my hand and led me to the cliff gently pushing me against a smooth rock wall. He lifted me up pulling my thighs around him as he pushed into me.

"Why—?" I started.

"Why what?" he asked between pushes.

"Why did it take me so long to get those clothes off?"

The rocky wall was going to leave a speckly imprint on my back but I didn't care. I didn't care about anything except that hot pleasure between my legs. I gripped Jim's hips so tightly I thought he might complain, but he was too busy burying himself in me, pressing me into the wall. My arms around Jim never wanted to let him go. His lovebite in my neck sent shivers through me as he came in me with deep thrusts that had us both crying out with pleasure.

When we relaxed and my legs slid down to the ground, I almost couldn't stand. The shudders of pleasure were still throbbing through me. I held onto Jim for a few moments more and we let our hearts pound against each other.

"I love you, Andrea," Jim whispered into my ear. "But now, for the surprise."

"You mean this wasn't it?"

Jim reached for the black bag and pulled out a bottle of shampoo. He took my hand and led me to the back of the waterfall. The spray of water felt so refreshing after the buildup of heat. Jim squeezed some shampoo into his hand and massaged it into my hair. It felt heavenly. I took a bit of shampoo from the lather in my hair and did the same for him. We soaped each other up from top to bottom, not missing any part of our bodies. Then came the grand finale as we stepped into the flow of water. We gasped and shrieked from the shock of the cold as the tumbling water pummeled us. Then we stepped out into the sunshine totally clean and rejuvenated, and so much in love.

Chapter 47

Monique!" Sarah ran down the ramp of the float where I was tying up George's water taxi for the day. "I need to talk to you." She was all out of breath.

"Just a sec." I turned to give my two passengers a hand out of the boat and onto the float.

"Thanks for the ride, Monique," they said as I handed them their bags and touched the peak of my cap.

I turned to Sarah. "What's got you so 'ot? Somet'ing wrong?"

"The cops came back a second time to ask if I know where Robert is."

"So? Do you?"

"No! I told them Finn Bay, but they said his boat was gone." She looked like she was going to cry.

"What's de big deal?" I shrugged. "So 'e left. So what?"

"You don't understand. Last night just before we went into the hotel for supper, he saw the Serenity leaving, and it bothered him the whole evening. I didn't let on I'd seen Andrea, but he got really antsy. He kept at me until I admitted I'd seen Andrea and talked to her briefly. Then he drilled me with questions. 'Why didn't you tell me? Why were they here? Where were they going? What did you say to them?'"

I shook my head. "My God! 'e is really crazy."

"I know! I told him I didn't say anything. Only that I told Andrea he was with me now. I asked him why he couldn't see that he's lost Andrea forever. She will never come back to him." She stopped to wipe away tears. "That's when he jumped up from the table. 'We're done!' he said. 'How could you not tell me Andrea was here?' His precious fucking Andrea. He still wants her. He's nuts. He's, he's ... obsessed with her. And then he stomped out and stuck me with the bill."

"But why are you telling me all dis?" I asked.

"I know you care about Andrea." She hesitated and then looked away. "And okay, I care about Robert."

"So?"

"So I thought maybe you could somehow get a message to Andrea and Jim and warn them that Robert is coming for them. I'm afraid someone is going to get hurt. Maybe between the two of them, they can convince him to back off and give up. Then maybe he'll come home." She shrugged and let her arms dangle limply by her sides.

"I don't see 'ow I can do dat. If I call dem on de radio Robert will know."

"Can't you go after them?" She pointed at George's boat. "Use the water taxi?"

"Get serious!" I said. "It's not my boat, you know."

"If you don't, somebody is going to get hurt. I just know it. You didn't see how his eyes glazed over and his jaw was so tight. It was creepy. And then just before he left the restaurant, he squinted his eyes almost shut. He looked so mad. When he jumped up I thought he was going to knock over the table. He was in such a blind rage and in a hurry to get going."

I crossed my arms over my chest and didn't say anything. Had to think about what to do. I could see that Sarah was feeling desperate. And she was probably right about Andrea being in danger—not to mention Jim.

Sarah made one last pitch. "I know you love Andrea. You don't want to see her get hurt, do you?"

I blew out the breath I'd been holding. "I will talk to George. See if I can borrow de boat for a few hours tomorrow. Dat's de best I can do."

"Thanks, Monique. I can come with you if you want."

"Dat's okay. I can 'andle it." *Much better wit'out you.*

George, I 'ave a big favour to ask." *I put on my sweetest smile.*

"Oh yeah? What's that? You want a day off?"

I laughed a little uncomfortably. I hadn't realized I would also need a day off along with the loan of the boat. "You remember my friend Andrea? She is on the Serenity and I have to warn her that she's in danger. Robert is coming for her. Sarah told me. I would like to borrow de taxi tomorrow for a few hours."

"What!?" George threw his arms in the air and then pointed to his head. "Are you crazy?"

I didn't say anything. Just waited.

"Why can't you just call her on the VHF?"

"Robert would 'ear it. You just 'ave to trust me. I only need it for a few hours. And of course I pay de fuel."

"But—"

"I even fill de tank when I am finished."

"But—"

"And I work for you two days for free."

"Okay."

I reached out my hand and George shook it. "One day free is good enough."

I grinned at George. "T'ank you so much."

"But you be bloody careful!"

The next day I threw my pack into the boat and drove over to the fuel dock to fill the water taxi's fuel tank with diesel. I brought an extra fuel caddy with me just in case. I had extra drinking water and enough food for two days. I should only be gone for a few hours but just in case, it was good to be prepared. I didn't know how far Jim and Andrea had gone and it might take me some extra time to check all the little bays and anchorages along the way.

Luckily the weather was fine. I wouldn't try it in bad weather with the small boat. It was pretty tough, but I had to remember its limitations and I needed to be aware of the weather forecast.

I headed out of Lund's harbour and scooted across to the Copelands first. I thought I heard Andrea say they might go there first. That was two days ago but maybe they decided to stay there a while. It's such a nice place. I wondered if Andrea remembered the time when we went there together and I taught her how to run an outboard motor. We had a great day that time. I sighed. Wish things had turned out differently, but Andrea wasn't gay and there was nothing either of us could do about it.

No boats at the Copelands, so I kept going up the channel and over towards Tenedos Bay. I did a quick buzz around Galley Bay on the way just to make sure they weren't in there. No wonder they didn't stop there. Nothing to do and you couldn't even go ashore there because of the big dogs that cruise the beach. They belonged to the "back to the land" guy who lived in the single cabin in there. He was probably a harmless American draft dodger from years ago who just wanted to be left alone. Nobody was going to pay him any surprise visit with those big dogs patrolling.

On to Tenedos Bay. Two sailboats pulled at their anchor lines in the gentle breeze. No fishboats. I went between the little islands and kept going to check Prideaux Haven. A huge white yacht was dropping its anchor. A young crewman was unwinding the anchor chain while a white-haired woman in a white blouse and white dress pants with a gold belt, eyed him up and down while she held onto the back of a deck chair and sucked nicotine through her cigarette holder. *Wonder what's going on there?*

The opening into Prideaux Haven is very narrow, so I was surprised to see the yacht, but with the modern navigation programs, it was amazing how big boats could maneuver into small places. I did a quick loop of the bay, but there was no Serenity.

On I went, first retracing my path towards Tenedos Bay and then turning northward. I passed the place where Robert had his cabin. Nothing but a charred foundation was left. No boat tied to the tiny dock in front of the place. Just as well. I didn't really want to run into Robert. The guy was dangerous.

By late afternoon I got as far as Teakerne Arm. If they weren't there, I would have to give up and turn back. The days were long but I would have to think about getting home before dark. I had about three hours to spare before I had to head back.

As I entered the long arm of water, I spotted a troller way up ahead. I slowed the boat to a crawl and got out the binoculars. At last, there it was. The Serenity lay anchored up ahead. No other boats in sight.

I pulled alongside the troller and tossed a line to Jim who stood there wide-eyed and grinning.

"Andrea, come out here," he called. "Look who's here." He gave me a hand up and I stood aboard the Serenity, hugging first Jim and then a surprised Andrea.

Chapter 48

I was shocked to see Monique. "What are YOU doing here?" I squealed. I nearly crushed her with my hug and she responded in kind.

When I pulled away from her, it hit me that she shouldn't be here. "Really. What *are* you doing here?"

Jim, at least, had his wits about him and asked Monique to sit down. "Would you like a cup of coffee?"

"Love one! T'ank you," she said.

"It's great to see you, Monique, but I don't understand. Why are you here with the water taxi? Did you have a customer?" I asked.

She took the coffee Jim handed her. "Sarah wanted me to come and warn you about Robert."

A chilly cloud seemed to hover over the boat as she continued to tell us the story about Robert having disappeared after fighting with Sarah in the restaurant. Sarah thought Robert was obsessed with getting me back and she was afraid that Jim and I were danger. She also hoped we could convince Robert to give up and come back to her. *As if that would ever work!* Sarah didn't care a whit about me; she was just hoping to get Robert back. She was welcome to him, but first she had to find him.

"We haven't seen any sign of a gray boat," Jim said. "Did you? On your way up here?"

"No, and dat's de strange t'ing. But den, 'e could be anywhere. It's a big coast with lots of little bays to duck into and islands to 'ide behind."

"Or he might have continued on straight north without stopping to lurk around in any bays."

"Dat's true. Well, I did not want you to be 'urt. Just be careful."

"We appreciate what you've done, Monique," said Jim. "We'll definitely take more precautions now that we know."

"I've just whipped up some supper for us and there's enough to feed a small army. You'll stay, won't you?" I asked.

"I'd love to stay and eat wit' you, and we can 'ave dat visit we did not 'ave in Lund. But den I 'ave to leave to give me time to get back before dark. Dis boat she goes pretty fast, but still, I need to allow time so I am not panic to get back."

I got up to bring us our supper. "That makes good sense, Monique. We'll eat right away and you'll have plenty of time to get back."

We laughed a lot in spite of the chilling news that Monique had brought us, and too soon she had to say goodbye. I hugged her tightly. "Thank you so much for going to so much trouble to warn us. Don't worry though. We'll be just fine."

"Drive safely," Jim called as we waved to her from the Serenity's deck.

That night, after our waterfall shower we should have slept like babies, but Monique's visit had us sitting up late talking about all sorts of possibilities. We agreed that we would be safest from Robert on the Serenity.

I don't think Jim slept much that night either as he had set the alarm for five but was up before it rang. He had the coffee made before I got dressed.

He handed me a cup. "I thought we'd enjoy the quiet of the bay while we have our coffee on deck. We'll have enough of that engine noise today. It's going to be a good day's run, maybe seven hours or so."

"Where are we headed?" I asked.

"Knox Bay, I hope. It's a good anchorage unless it's really blowing southeast, which it isn't going to. I think if Robert is in these waters, we'll be better off just heading straight north, sticking to the Serenity, rather than hanging out in these holiday places where we might leave the boat to go for rides in the skiff."

"Shouldn't we get going then, if it's a long run?" He seemed quite relaxed and not in a rush to go anywhere.

"We've got some time. I'd rather go with the tide if we can. By the time we have our coffee and a bit of breakfast we can think about warming up the engine and pulling the anchor." Jim went into the wheelhouse and turned the VHF to the weather channel. I could hear the sound of a voice giving the marine weather. When Jim stepped back out onto the deck, he announced, "At least the weather's great."

Later in the day, Jim set the boat on autopilot. While he had a quick nap, all I had to do was watch for logs or any big seaweed mats and push the dodge button if anything came close to the boat. As I steered—well, watched the boat steer itself—I studied the marine atlas. Jim had penciled in some spots that were good for crabbing, but as we weren't stopping to throw out any crab rings, all I could think of was that it wouldn't be a good place to fall overboard. I could just picture those spiderlike creatures pulling pieces of meat off me with their pincers and nibbling on me. A shudder passed over me. I had too much of an imagination sometimes.

I thought back to the very real time I went out in Robert's skiff with him to put the crab rings out and then to collect them later with crabs in them. It was one of the most horrible days of my life. He was so sarcastic and took pleasure in making me look foolish—the way he lurched the skiff ahead when I wasn't expecting it and I fell backwards. He thought it was funny that my jeans got soaked, while I was humiliated and in pain where my tailbone landed on the oar that lay in the bottom of the skiff.

"Bastard!" I muttered. "Disgusting piece of shit."

"What did I do?" Jim's voice by my shoulder made me jump.

"Oh! Have a good nap? That was quick."

"I don't need much time. Fifteen minutes and I'm as good as new," he said. "But what was all that cussing about? Did I do something?"

"No ... of course not." I reached over to stroke his cheek. "I was just remembering a bad day with Robert. Sorry."

Jim hugged me. "You don't need to apologize. I know you had a hard time with him. I'm really glad you're away from him."

I laughed. "Not as glad as I am." I slid off the captain's bench and let Jim take over the wheel. I was glad for the Nobeltec chart on the monitor that showed such detail. Coming up to Blind Channel, it looked a bit narrow on the atlas map and I was nervous as we turned into it from Cordero Channel. But like so many other tight places I had been with both Robert and Jim on their boats, it turned out to be a piece of cake.

"Look there, Jim." I pointed towards shore. "In that little bay, there's a fuel up place and a wharf. You mentioned we have to get fuel soon. We could get it there."

"I stopped there once, and they sell fuel all right, but you'd think they were selling gold nuggets. Way too much money! We can get our fuel at Port Hardy. We have to get some groceries anyway before we head up the coast. There'll be nothing much after that until we get to Prince Rupert."

Jim had done this route before, many times, and I trusted him completely. We carried on and in a short time, we entered the bigger water highway of Johnstone Strait. No sign of Robert in any of the little waterways and none here either. If he was on our trail, I'd seen no sign of him. Unless he had gone ahead of us and was waiting to ambush us somewhere. I'd have to keep a close watch.

It was only about an hour before we approached the entrance to Knox Bay. The place was empty except for a small sailboat at the south end of it. Jim headed for the far end of the bay. "I'll be glad to turn off the engine," he said. "It's been a long day. I'm dropping tired. Want to go get the anchor ready?"

That meant I should pull some of the heavy chain off the huge spool and pile it up at the bow, so that when the anchor was kicked overboard, the chain would follow quickly and easily without being slowed down by resistance from the spool. Once it got going over the side, the rest free-spooled quickly enough to lie on the bottom and add weight to the anchor.

I was about to leave the wheelhouse when I pointed at the depth sounder. "Jim! The bottom's coming up fast!"

"Holy shit!" He pulled on the gear shift and slammed it into reverse. "Fuck! I forgot it's shallow for a long way from the shore on this side." As soon as we got a couple more fathoms under the hull, he turned the boat and pushed the gear lever forward again. "Oh my God!" He gave it a shot of fuel and gunned it out of the shallows, leaving a cloud of black smoke in the air. At least he knew what to do in a hurry.

Farther out he did his usual reconnaissance circle while I went out to prepare the anchor. I sat on the skylight cover with my foot ready to kick out the heavy anchor and waited for Jim's signal.

When he put the boat in reverse, he called, "Okay! Kick her out and keep your feet out of the way."

Once the anchor was out far enough, Jim turned the handle to put the brake on the big spool to stop the rest of the anchor line from going out. Then he gave the boat one little shot of fuel to set the hook before shutting down the engine.

In the sudden stillness we looked at each other and breathed a long sigh. Jim hugged me. "This is what happens when you're overtired and distracted. What would I do without you?"

I smiled into his chest. "Probably run aground."

"For sure I'd founder. Better stick with me."

Chapter 49

The next day was long, even after waiting for the tide to carry us along. Inevitably, that tide would change and we'd be bucking it for a few hours, but for the first while at least, we had a light southeast breeze giving us an extra push with the tide and we made good time.

"We've been lucky," Jim said. "The tide ebbs to the north here and the southeast is on our tail. It'll get us past Kelsey Bay. That can be a nasty bit of water in the wrong combination of wind and tide."

"I can believe it," I said. "Even now, the tideline is all foamy, running away carrying bits of logs and bark. There must be a lot of logging around here."

"Used to be a big thing. Mostly smaller operations now. But those logs you see are floating around because the tide was extra high yesterday and a lot of the beached logs got lifted up and now they're floating out here. Watch out for any that are in our way. We don't want to hit a log."

"What would happen? I mean I know it's not good, but wouldn't it just be pushed out of the way?"

"Depends on how you hit it. If it's a smallish log and you hit it at an angle, it would just glance off. No harm done. But if you hit it crosswise, it might go under the boat and it could wreck your propeller blades—twist them if not break them."

"What if you hit one end-on?"

"If it was a big one, or we were going fast, it could stave your planks in and you'd take on water."

I shuddered. "That wouldn't be good."

"You got that right. So keep an eye out for logs and use the dodge button if it looks like we might be too close to anything bigger than a few feet long."

Late that day we pulled into Sointula. A scan of the boats tied to the floats told me that Robert was nowhere near. At least, I didn't think he was. Jim and I would have to check more carefully once we tied up. The only way he could be here waiting for us was if he had slipped past us when we were anchored at Tenedos Bay and Teakerne Arm. Monique thought he might be following us, but she could have been mistaken. Robert might just be fed up with Sarah and be heading north to fish just like we were. But you never really knew with him. He might still be trying to get me to come back and one thing I knew for sure, he was always full of nasty surprises. For now, I was pretty sure we were safe.

We tied to the dock at the fish buyers in Port Hardy early the next day after a short run from Sointula. It was a cleanup and maintenance day. We wanted to be well prepared for all possibilities. If we ran into Robert, it might take longer to get to Prince Rupert. We'd seen no sign of him and I was feeling more relaxed all the time. I wanted to believe he was tired of the whole thing. I know I sure was.

We got diesel for the boat and Jim did an oil change. He liked to keep on top of that. Said it made the engine run better and last longer. I liked that he was so conscientious about keeping the boat in good condition. Made me feel safer being on it too. It was that much less likely that we would have a breakdown during fishing season when every day counted. The Department of Fisheries and Oceans only allowed so many days of salmon fishing and any missed days could mean a lot of missed money. And a lot of that money was needed to pay the expenses that kept racking up regardless of whether you caught fish or not.

We walked in to town once the boat was fueled up and we had filled the fresh water tanks. We'd get our exercise with a half hour walk to the store, get our groceries, and take a taxi back.

In the morning, we left Vancouver Island, crossing the open water of Queen Charlotte Strait towards the mainland coast. We were in a good headspace knowing the boat was in fine shape, and still we had not seen Robert.

"Where do you think we'll end up tonight?"

"I think a handy anchorage for us tonight will be Safety Cove on Calvert Island."

"Oh yes, we were in there—"

"I know. Last year, when you were on Robert's boat and I was tagging along."

"You don't know how badly I wished I could swim across to your boat that night," I said.

"We would have met in the middle because I was thinking the same thing."

"We both would have ended up being shot by that maniac."

"Well, let's hope he's out of the picture now. Let's try to enjoy our trip up north. We have great weather and we'll be snug in Safety Cove tonight. No point in staying longer to go ashore though."

"I wasn't thinking about it but why not?"

"Wolves. There's a lot of wolves in that area. All up the coast, for that matter. I saw them from the skiff one time when I stopped to do a bit of sport fishing—a whole family of them."

"I think I'll stay right here on the boat with you."

We left Safety Cove about 5:30 the next morning threading our way through the maze of islands and inlets along BC's rugged coast.

I marked down the main waypoints on paper while Jim entered them on the Nobeltec program. That amazing program would be our main guide but we both still felt it was important to use the charts to know where we were. You never knew when a computer might give out and if that were our only guide, we'd be lost.

Fitzhugh Sound was like a freeway, a huge, wide water highway. Through several channels we went, until we came out at Milbanke Sound. It looked like the open ocean here, and in a way, I suppose it was. It even felt like the real ocean with the swells coming in, just like when we were on the west coast of the Queen Charlottes last year. There's a feeling that comes over a person. It seems to ride in on the swells and call to the soul, which brought John Masefield's words to me:

"I must go down to the seas again, to the lonely sea and the sky ...," and I understood the draw that the sea could have on a soul.

Right now, if we had headed in a direction somewhere near 200 degrees, we probably would have kept going all the way to China. But we could bypass Milbanke Sound by going through tiny Reid Passage and on up Mathieson

Channel. It was here I got a whiff of something not quite right. That brought me back to reality in a hurry.

"Do you smell something?" I asked.

Jim didn't even glance up from writing in his journal. "Like what?"

I walked around the galley, sniffing the air. "Kind of warm and sweet."

"You baking something?"

"No, not that kind of sweet. More like metallic sweet, gasoline, or alcohol sweet, but not that pleasant. Can't you smell it?"

Jim put the journal back onto the helm. "Yeah. Now I do." He glanced at the panel of gauges and buttons behind him.

"The water temperature is pretty high. Must be losing coolant or...."

I jumped at the sound of a bell ringing at such a volume that it hurt my ears. Then I realized I was standing right beside the alarm. The jittery feeling spread instantly to my stomach and out to all the nerve endings of my arms and legs.

"What's happening?" I shouted over the deafening noise. I knew something was terribly wrong. "Are we on fire?"

Jim took the boat out of gear and throttled back. He leapt up, lifted up the floorboard beside the bench, and removed the stairs that led down to the fo'c'sle. Behind the stairs was access to the engine room.

"It's steamy in here! I think we've got a coolant leak. Fill a pot with water from the sink and pour it into the expansion tank!"

"Expansion—?" I stood like a deer caught in the headlights.

He stuck his head up and pointed at the small aluminum tank that was right under the passenger seat. "Right there, dammit! Add water to it. And pull that cable by the door to choke off the engine. We have to shut it down while I fix the leak!"

How was I supposed to know it was the expansion tank, whatever the hell that was? It was just a metal box, for Chrissake.

The oil pressure gauge rang like a shrill old-fashioned telephone when the engine stopped and the pressure dropped. I slammed my hand into the button to shut it off.

While I rushed to fill a pot with water, slopping it all over, partly from nerves and partly because I was pissed off, Jim climbed out from downstairs and unscrewed the cap of the tank. He stuck a long-handled wooden spoon into it. "Bone dry," he said. "Keep pouring water in here while I go below and fix the leak."

"Yes, boss." I spat at him and spun around to fill another pot of water.

As the water filled the expansion tank, and Jim was below in the engine room, I kept a lookout to make sure we weren't drifting into trouble. Luckily we were in a huge channel and no traffic was nearby. I didn't like the feeling of drifting aimlessly, turning in directions we didn't want to go, being taken by the tide.

I took a rag and cleaned up the water that my shaking hands had spilled on the floor and on the counter. My nerves still buzzed and jittered.

I heard Jim grunting and swearing under my feet. "Keep a watch for traffic," he called up.

"We're fine. I'm watching." *Not hitting anything or drifting onto rockpiles. Not yet, anyway. But for how long could we drift like this with no control over the boat?*

After what seemed like an hour but was only probably twenty minutes, Jim came up into the wheelhouse. His face was red and beaded with sweat. Smears of black grease covered much of his face. He took off his glasses and handed them to me. "D'you mind giving them a wipe for me? I don't think they'd get cleaner with me doing it."

I took them wordlessly and gave them a wipe and handed them back.

"Something wrong?" he asked.

I just shook my head and turned away.

He reached up and pushed the start button. The engine caught right away and as Jim revved it up, we watched the temperature gauge drop.

"Whew!" he said. "We'll be okay." He looked at the Nobeltec monitor. "We've drifted off course a bit but nothing too serious."

"Now," he said, reaching for me, "what's the problem?"

"Nothing." I pulled away.

"It's not nothing, or you wouldn't be acting weird."

"Well, maybe I'm weird, but you're too much like Robert." There. I got it out.

"What!?" He grabbed my arm. I looked down at his hand and back into his face. He let go.

"See what I mean? Men! They're all the same. Power and control is all you want."

Jim stood there looking dazed. "Where in the hell is this coming from?"

"You yelled at me."

"Well, you're yelling now!" he said. "So you're allowed to yell but I'm not?"

"Just because I don't know everything about the boat you don't have to yell at me. You don't know everything either. Look at how you nearly ran us aground at Knox

Bay. And you knew there were bears at Tenedos Bay and still you took me ashore there." I knew I was babbling nonsense, but I was hurt. "I don't like being yelled at."

"I'm sorry I yelled, okay? It's just ... we had an emergency and you just stood there." He shrugged. "And I hate being compared to Robert. That's not fair. Dammit, Andrea, I'm nothing like him and you know it."

I hung my head and felt ashamed at my outburst. "Yes, you're right. I'm sorry."

Jim reached for me and this time I didn't push him away. I sniffled into his neck and held him tight. "I'm sorry," I said again.

"Me too." He kissed my hair and rubbed my back. "I'll try never to yell at you again."

"And I won't call you Robert again."

"Yeah, that was really below the belt."

"I know. Okay, truce?"

"Truce."

"So what's our situation with the boat?" I asked.

"Just a pinhole of water spraying. Must have been leaking for a long time, but only squirting hard with the engine running. That's why I didn't notice it before." He wiped his brow with the back of his hand. "Hot down there."

It felt so good to get the boat back on track and under power—to have control again.

"How did you fix it?"

"It's only a quick fix. Just a few tight wraps of electrician's tape for now. It's going to need a better fix once we get anchored up."

"Will we be okay until we get where we're going?"

"We should be near Jackson's Passage in the next half hour or so. We can anchor just inside at Rescue

Bay and I can do a more permanent repair job there once the engine has cooled off."

Sure enough, in about half an hour we turned into a beautiful bay near the east entrance of Jackson's Passage. Rescue Bay was such a pretty place! At the farther end of the bay the shore looked reedy which was quite unusual to see on this rocky coastline. Not a boat in sight. Just the way I liked it. Safer that way.

Jim did his usual loop of the area to check the depth, and then we dropped the hook, and shut off the engine. Except for the time spent drifting to deal with the overheating problem, we had been listening to that engine since early that morning at Safety Cove. Since there was no sign of a gray troller, we took off our shoes and fell into our bunks for a desperately needed nap. Supper and engine repairs could wait.

Chapter 50

Waking up in paradise was good for the soul after all the long tiring runs. We'd seen no sign of Robert and were feeling almost as if our lives were back to normal. I was glad to have a safe anchorage so I could take the time to fix the leaky water hose. Some tightly wrapped strips of rubber inner tube fastened on with hose clamps should get me to Prince Rupert where I could get a spare piece of hose. Luckily, I had spares of almost everything I might need for minor breakdowns. Except a piece of hose for the cooling system.

Andrea sat on the deck reading a book while I fixed the hose. We had tiptoed around each other last night after our big fight and she seemed as cautiously optimistic as I was today.

I had the repair job done in about half an hour and soon we were ready to move on. I could have stayed a bit longer, but I knew I had a lot of things to take care of once I got to Prince Rupert and Masset. To Andrea it was more of a holiday at this stage, and I had tried to make it sound like that, but the truth was, I was getting antsy to be ready for the season. I still had to get more gear tied, take on fresh ice in Masset, top up the fuel once we got there, and talk to some of the local fishermen to find out what was happening, if anything was new since last summer's season. I had about a week to spare after we would arrive, but that would go quickly, and I had to allow for any last minute repairs that might need doing.

The weather was another factor. Up in this neck of the woods, the wind could come up fast and it could blow for three days in a row. If that happened, we could be sitting outside of Prince Rupert waiting for Hecate Strait to calm down before a small boat like ours dared risk the all-day crossing to the Charlottes.

Probably all the uncertainties and the stress of having such a long list of things I had to do was what made me so quick to raise my voice yesterday. Monique's warning also put me on edge more than usual. I'd have to be more careful. Andrea didn't deserve that and it wouldn't do either of us any good. I made up my mind to try not to let things get to me so easily.

Reluctantly, I started up the engine for another long day's run. I went below to check on the water hose now that the engine was running. It seemed fine. We'd be in Prince Rupert in a couple of days. I would try to end up in Khutze Inlet tonight. But first we had to get through this narrow ditch called Jackson's Passage.

"Have you been through here with Robert?" I asked Andrea. I hated to mention his name.

"No. I think we stayed in Klemtu on the way north. It's near here isn't it?"

"Yeah, just across the next big channel. You'll see when we go by. But first, get ready for a tight squeeze through Jackson's Passage." The engine was warmed up and the monitor was running with Nobeltec showing the map of this area up close. I needed it to be nice and big so I could follow the ditch through to the other side where it opened up into Finlayson Channel, another big water freeway.

As we chugged through the passage, Andrea's fingers gripped the helm ever more tightly. I patted her hand. "Don't worry. Nobeltec will take us through."

Her face was white and set in a tight mask. "I feel like someone is squeezing my throat. This ditch is getting smaller all the time. Are you sure boats are supposed to go through here?"

"Bigger boats than ours go through here all the time," I said. *I just hope we don't meet any coming from the other direction.*

"I can almost reach out and touch the banks." Andrea's hands crossed over her chest. "Oh my God, this is stressful."

I patted her shoulder. "Don't worry. We'll be fine. See it's opening up wider already. We'll be out in no time."

She laughed nervously. "Can't be soon enough for me."

Just about then we came out into Finlayson Channel.

"Lots of room now," I said.

"The fog sure is thick out here. Just a mist back there, but out here it's thick as pea soup. Is this safe, driving along when we can't see where we're going?"

"I turned on the radar. You have a look and let us know if there's any other traffic." That was another thing I'd have to deal with this winter. My radar was an ancient thing that had come with the boat. It was really outdated, but it had a powerful range. Still, you had to put your face down into a mask to block out the light and look at the screen that way. The modern ones all had a monitor you could look at like a computer screen.

"I've never done much radar stuff. Robert never trusted me to do it right."

"Well, there's nothing to it. Boats will show up as a little blip on the screen. As that line goes around in a circle, if it sweeps across anything solid in the water, it will show up as a dot and you'll see it. The concentric circles on the screen tell you how far away the boat is.

Okay?" I stuck my head onto the face rest and had a quick look, then pointed at it for Andrea to do the same.

"Yeah, okay. I'll try." She stuck her head on the radar's rubber face rest. "No blips at all."

We were nearing the center of the channel when Andrea put her head down for another look at the radar screen. Her voice sounded muffled in the mask as she asked, "What does it mean when there's a big square right in the center of the screen?"

My brow wrinkled and I tried to think what she could be talking about. "What? Let me see." She backed out of the way and I stuck my face into the radar. "Holy shit!" I yelled.

I looked up through the windshield and there, looming in front of us was a gigantic wall. I cut the throttle and turned the wheel sharply to the right, gave it some juice and did the fastest, tightest turn I've ever made in my life. I looked up at the hull of the cruise ship *Nieuw Amsterdam* and saw a line of passengers at the rail near the top. Some of them waved and others pointed at us. Worst of all, some took pictures.

We narrowly escaped a collision with the cruise ship but the worst was yet to come as we bounced up and down over its wake. I didn't have the poles down so we flailed from port to starboard and back many times before the seas calmed down again.

"I'm sorry," Andrea cried. "I'm really sorry." She picked up the thermos bottle and a mug that had bounced onto the floor.

"Hey, it's okay. It's my responsibility." I tried to stop my voice from shaking. Now that the danger was over, the adrenaline was still coursing through my veins and I sat down in the captain's bench so Andrea wouldn't notice my quivering knees.

"Don't ever ask me to go on a cruise ship," Andrea said. "This is as close as I ever want to get to one."

Andrea poured us each a cup of newly made coffee and dug out some cookies we had bought in Port Hardy. "I think we need a treat for surviving that near miss," she said.

I gave a little snort. "Why do they call it a near miss when it really is a near hit?"

"I don't know." Andrea shrugged her shoulders. "Stupid, isn't it? Anyway it's more for airplanes, I think."

"Speaking of airplanes, a few years ago a small plane crashed on this island we're going by now. That's Cone Island. Klemtu is just on the other side of it on Swindle Island."

"Was anyone killed? What happened?"

"Well, they found the wreckage but no one was in it. The passengers left a note in the plane, saying they were going to walk out looking for help and they were never seen again."

"Didn't you say it was an island though?"

"Yes, that one there." I pointed at Cone Island on the map. "Not a trace was found. They figure the wolves must have got them. There wouldn't be much left of them. I always thought it was odd that no clothing was found either, but over the years it would have disintegrated with the weather. It gets very windy here too."

Andrea shuddered. "I know. I was stuck in the cabin through many a blow."

"Yes, you would know how wild it can get out here in the winter." I checked the radar again just to be sure it was clear. A small boat was some distance behind us. Not close enough to worry about. At least, I didn't think so…. Nothing coming our way. I'd have to keep an eye on the boat behind us but for now I would keep it to myself.

"That fog seems to be lifting," Andrea said. "How about if I make us some breakfast, now that the excitement is over?"

"How about if I make it instead? You can sit and mind the helm. It's wide open here so you don't have to be too particular about watching for shallow spots. Just keep an eye out for logs and seaweed mats. Later on we'll get to some narrower spaces and I can take over then."

Andrea smiled at me. "Sure. Sounds great. I like it when a man makes breakfast for me."

I put the frying pan on the stove to warm up while I went out on deck to lift the hatch cover and get the eggs from the shelf just above the hold full of ice. I grabbed the cheese and butter while I was out there. I looked toward the stern and the waters beyond. The small boat I'd seen on the radar wasn't even visible. Could be any fishboat heading north or a sailboat. A lot of Americans sailed to Alaska through here.

I cut a couple of slices of bread and laid them right on the heavy cast iron stovetop to toast. A dab of butter was slowly melting in the pan as it heated up. The kettle was always on the stove—our hot water supply—so I set up the cone filter on top of the coffee pot. I had the coffee in the filter and poured the water a bit at a time.

"How's it going up there?" I did a quick scan out the front windows.

"Good." Andrea pointed. "There's something in the water up there, but I can't see what it is yet. Anyway, I'm sure we'll pass by it."

I put the toast on our plates and cracked four eggs into the pan and put a lid on it. "We can have a cup of coffee while we're waiting for the eggs," I said. "I'll just go out and get your cream."

"Oh, I—" Andrea sounded flustered. "Jim?"

I put the hatch cover down and stepped back into the wheelhouse.

"The wheel doesn't seem to be responding," she said in a tight, panicky voice. "There's a pretty big—"

A clunking noise rumbled along under the hull. I felt the vibration in my feet. I lurched forward, shoved Andrea out of the way, and pulled the gear and throttle lever up together, powering down and taking it out of gear at the same time. An awful thud hit the propeller and I ran back out on deck, pushing Andrea out of the way a second time. Behind the boat, a huge log popped up and floated away in our diminishing wake.

Carefully, I pushed the gear lever forward to engage it again. I listened for any odd sounds or vibrations. We seemed to be all right, so I pushed the throttle forward and got us going again, still listening for any strange vibrations. "I think we're okay."

"I'm sorry," Andrea said. "I tried to turn the steering wheel, but it didn't respond. It was just free-wheeling."

"That's because it's on auto-pilot. You have to switch the button to "P" for Power steer if you want to steer with the wheel."

"I thought the "P" by the switch stood for Pilot. I know that doesn't make sense because we were on auto-pilot already, but I just got mixed up when I panicked."

I shook my head and rolled my eyes. *Women!* But Andrea looked so seriously flustered and sorry that I turned away to hide the smile I couldn't keep off my face.

"What were you doing with the gear lever?"

"I had to get the engine out of gear to stop the propeller from spinning—at least not quite as fast—or the log could have done some expensive damage to it. Sorry I pushed you, but it had to be done in a hurry or it could have ended badly. You okay?"

She nodded and wrapped her arms around herself protectively.

"Don't worry about it. We're okay." I glanced over at the table. "I'll have to pour us new coffees though. Looks like I spilled it when I was dashing up to the helm. And I'd better rescue those eggs."

We ate our breakfast at the helm then, watching the miles swish away under the hull as we headed north. "I think our holiday time is almost over, but I'm glad we don't have to rush for the rest of the trip to Masset. It's good to have plenty of time."

"I know what you mean." Andrea nodded. "And I'd be really surprised if Robert went to all the trouble to chase after us this far. I haven't seen any sign of him so I think we're okay."

I didn't answer right away, thinking about that boat on the radar screen.

"Don't you think so, Jim?" Andrea looked for me to agree, already nodding for me.

"We're probably not even going to see him. There was a little boat in the distance this morning but there are so many boaters traveling north this time of year. You've seen them going by us. Holiday sailors. The one that didn't catch up to us is probably a very slow boat. Could have been a tug and barge. Anyway, I'm pretty sure we don't need to worry about Robert."

"I don't mind if the holiday part is over. It's not as warm up this way anyway. Amazing what a few miles can do. Ever since we crossed from Port Hardy, let's say since Safety Cove, it's been cooler."

"That's how it is most of the time. Fishermen heading north call it going under the cloud."

"Still beautiful though."

"This afternoon you'll see what "really beautiful" looks like. I can't wait to show you this place. And in spite of all these steep mountains around, we'll be able to go for a walk."

"Sounds great. It'll be good to get off the boat for a while." She looked up to see my reaction. "I mean I like the boat, but it'll be nice to walk a bit."

"I knew what you meant. I feel the same way. We should be there by early afternoon. That'll give us time to walk and explore a bit. Not much traffic along here at all, so we should have the whole place to ourselves."

Chapter 51

After the long day's run, I was really happy when Jim turned the Serenity into Khutze Inlet. At first I thought it was named after the birds—coots, which would have made sense as there were so many of them—but then I saw it on the map and realized it was spelled differently. It was a quiet little anchorage. The sailboats we'd seen had continued on and we had the place to ourselves. The bend at the head of it gave extra shelter from the wind and made it seem quiet and cozy, cut off from the rest of the world. Mountains all around added to that feeling. Just Jim and me in our own little world. And now he was promising me a beautiful trip ashore. We still had half the afternoon to check out the head of the inlet where a river entered it flowing from the mountains beyond.

"Hop into the skiff. We'll just take our basic survival kit in a pack and that'll be all we need. We won't be that long, but I promise you'll love it." Jim was already in the skiff and he steadied it against the side of the Serenity while I got in. "We could row in but it'll save time to use the outboard. Hate to spoil the stillness with the motor noise but it'll just be for a short run to shore. Also easier to go a little way up the mouth of the river using the motor."

The place was as picturesque as a calendar photo. The bright blue of the water changed to green in the bay. Reflections of the distant snow-capped mountains made it seem twice as scenic. Against all the blues and greens of the water and the hills, the range of gold and yellow of the marsh grasses contrasted beautifully.

After I climbed out of the skiff, the first few steps were muddy and my feet sank into the riverbank where the grasses met the mud. "I'm glad you reminded me to wear my boots."

"In boating it's almost always the best choice of footwear," Jim said. He tied the skiff to the top of the roots of a toppled snag. It would be safe there. That old log wasn't going anywhere. We walked across a huge meadow of coarse, yellow grass that lay on its side as if the whole place was windswept, but of course it was the tide that had flattened it. Once in a while there were long zig-zagging cracks in the earth where the tide had run in rivulets, forming creeks that were now dry because the tide was out. Often I could jump across these gaps, but we walked across a couple that were as wide as twenty feet.

The smell of the tidal flat was an intoxicating mixture of salty sea and marijuana. I inhaled and felt giddy with happiness. I was totally surrounded by nature. Not a hint of anything manmade.

I found a skull of what might have been a small deer half buried in the mud and wondered what its story was. A fearful thought struck me. "Jim! Are there grizzlies here?"

"I've got bear spray, and anyway, the bears are all up in the hills this time of year. Later in the summer they'll come down for the salmon, but not right now."

What if there were wolves around here? I didn't want to ask Jim. He'd think I was getting really paranoid, and I wanted him to think—to know—that I was enjoying the outing.

He spoke so confidently, I believed him, and yet, I couldn't help wondering if some of the depressions in the mud of the rivulets might be bear paw prints. My imagination was not always my friend.

"Look at these flowers, Jim. Aren't they precious?" I looked for him and he had wandered over to the edge of a back eddy of the small river.

"I think the Canada geese come in here. I see some of their tracks in the mud," he said. "We should check it out on our way home in the fall."

And so we walked from one point of interest to the next until we were quite far up the long, grassy field that ended with a few deciduous trees near the base of the mountains.

The sun was sinking low in the late afternoon. It would be light for a while yet, but with the mountains surrounding us, the sun dipped behind them earlier than usual. "We should start heading back," Jim said.

Some of the small rivulets were already filling with water as the tide came in, so we splashed through them, happy to have boots on. Each of the ditches had more water in them as we got closer towards the inlet and without comment we walked ever faster. As we came to one of the wider ditches, I tried to wade through, but after a few feet, the water reached the tops of my boots. I turned back to think about what to do. We looked for a way around or a narrower place where we might jump across, but this ditch was wide all along.

"Oh well, let's go for it. We'll get wet, but it's only water," I said.

But Jim put an arm out to stop me. "No sense both of us getting wet. I'll go and come back with the skiff. You go stand by the river's edge and wait for me."

I didn't like the idea of being left behind. What if Jim was wrong about the grizzlies? What if there were wolves? "No, let's both go."

I looked at the water that had come into the ditch. "It sure is coming in fast. We'd better go for it now before the whole place is flooded over." A sudden realization struck me that in a very short time we could be standing in the middle of a flooded plain, up to our necks in water.

It was then that we heard the sound of a motor and turned our attention to the river. A man was motoring up the river in a skiff. He pulled in to the bank and got out.

"Maybe one of the sailboats pulled in here after all," I said. "We can get a ride back to our skiff."

The man got out to tie up his skiff and then bent down to get something out of the boat. When he stood up and came towards us, shock and horror took over. I thought I was going to pee myself.

My heart pounded so hard I could feel it in my throat. "What are you doing here?" I yelled. Jim moved closer to me.

"Came to save a damsel in distress," Robert said. "Looks like the tide cut you off. I can give you a ride."

"Yeah, okay," Jim said. "We tied up the skiff just a little way down from here."

"I know the place, but I'm afraid it's not tied up there anymore." He had a nasty smirk on his face. I expected the worst. "I think it must have drifted away to the other side of the river. Seems to me it got caught up in a log jam on the other side. Pretty sure the motor was sunk."

"You sonofabitch." Jim's fists were clenched as he advanced on Robert, but he stopped when Robert raised the rifle.

"Stay right there. Now, Andrea, you come over here and get in the skiff," he ordered. "Do it now!" Robert's face looked wild. His eyes were intense and staring and his teeth showed as his lips pulled back in a snarl.

"No way. I'm not going anywhere with you. I'd rather drown here than get in that boat with you."

"Is that right? Well, you won't be drowning, but Jim here might if you don't park your sweet ass in that skiff. You'll get into it right now or I'll shoot him." Robert raised the rifle.

Come on, Andrea. Be brave. "You wouldn't kill Jim," I said, standing my ground.

"You're right, Andrea. I wouldn't kill him. I'd just blow out his kneecap and say the gun went off accidentally." His voice had been calm until then, making me realize he had it all figured out. Then he bellowed, "Now get in the fucking boat. I'm just itching for a reason to maim this bastard."

"Andrea, don't," Jim said. "He won't do it."

But Jim didn't know Robert like I did. I took a step towards the skiff. Jim grabbed my arm and pulled me back. Robert fired the rifle at our feet.

"Robert!" I shrieked. "Stop that!"

"You know what to do if you want me to stop."

I turned to Jim, and my voice trembled. "Please. I don't want him to have an excuse to kill you. We'll sort it out somehow but for now I have to go with him." I pulled away quickly and got in the skiff. "Okay, Robert. You've got me. Now put the gun down."

Robert lowered the gun slightly, just enough to allow him to get the motor started to take us down the river. "Don't worry about her, Jim. She'll be safe with me, but I don't know about you out here, stranded. Tsk! Tsk! That's a real shame. I'm anchored just around the bend from you. You can think about us while the tide comes in to swallow you up."

"Don't do this, Robert. At least bring him his skiff. You can't leave him. Please! Robert, please don't!" That was the extent of my pleading. The crash of Robert's hand across my face spun my head backwards and I fell into the bottom of the skiff. *Just like old times. You have to toughen up in a hurry, Andrea.* I pulled myself up and put on a brave face for Jim's sake, but I was filled with anguish to see him left behind. He stood on the bank raging impotently at Robert.

Chapter 52

I huddled in the front of Robert's skiff as far from him as possible, curled into a ball with my back to him. Knowing how sound carries across the surface of the water, I sobbed soundlessly as he sped back to the Hawkeye. I didn't want Jim to hear me crying. I knew he was already devastated. Not only would he be feeling guilty about me being in danger again, but he had good reason to fear for his own life. I really didn't care about any future beatings I might suffer at Robert's hands but I was inconsolably distressed about Jim being left to die. When we got to the Hawkeye, Robert took the painter, and holding onto the cap railing he put one leg up onto the guard rail and from there swung his other leg over onto the Hawkeye. He fastened the painter to the stanchion and pointed at the other tie-up line at the back of the skiff. "Toss me that line."

I didn't want his emotions to get out of control any more than they already were, so I handed it over to him and watched him tie it to the Hawkeye as well. He reached his hand down to help me aboard. I could have played hard to get but I had no chance of escaping so I held up my hand. He grabbed it and lifted me aboard as if I were weightless. I should actually have been weightless, considering how empty I felt inside.

He was probably angry and frustrated and hurt. I had no sympathy for him, but I had to try to win him over to buy myself some time. Maybe Jim could find a way to survive and come for me. But if I was honest with myself, I had to accept that there was little chance he would make it and it would be up to me to save myself.

I wanted to throw myself down on the deck and bawl my eyes out. Losing Jim. We'd been so happy. And yet, I thought about what a coward I had been when I lived with Robert and how I had promised myself I would never be that weak person again. I had to pull myself together. I took a few deep breaths and clenched my back teeth together while I found some inner resolve. I would cope. I would do better than cope. I would fight, but this time I would pick my battles and I would win. I thought of the ill treatment and injustices the women suffered in the movie, "Cold Mountain." They had also been bullied and abused by men who let power go to their heads. I wasn't a religious person, but I found some comfort in the Biblical line Nicole Kidman's character adapted: *When this war is over, there will be a reckoning.*

I had to move thoughts of self-pity over losing Jim to the back of my mind for the time being. Somehow I had to help end Robert's war on us and make him pay. There would be a reckoning, but first I had to try to save Jim. I couldn't jump into the skiff and rush out to save him. I had to fight the battle I could win. The first challenge was to get Robert calmed down and possibly even see reason. *Fat chance, but I have to try.* If I turned on just enough charm so he didn't get suspicious, maybe he would agree to go save Jim. And it had to be done in a hurry. That tide was moving in fast.

I let out a big sigh, so Robert could hear it. "Okay, Robert. You win. I'm here. Are you going to use me as your punching bag?"

"Andrea, don't be silly," he drawled. "How can you say that? Of course not. I only hit you a couple of times when you wouldn't do as you were told."

I looked at the deck at my feet. "I'm doing as I'm told now." I hoped that was enough submission to please him.

"Perfect." He pointed towards the door of the wheelhouse. "Why don't you go make us a cup of tea? You know where everything is."

I stepped over the raised sill into the wheelhouse and stood with my jaw hanging. The walls were covered in photos and magazine pictures of orchids. A potted orchid sat on the helm and another on the counter by the sink. Everywhere I looked were orchids. Sick, sick, sick.

I gave my head a shake and refocused. No outward sign of horror or amazement was going to give away my true thoughts or feelings. I reached for the teapot, found a teabag, and poured in the hot water from the kettle. I took down two mugs from the small corner cup rack and set them on the table.

Robert came in and sat at the table. I poured his tea and sat across from him just as I had done a year ago at this time before I ran away.

Robert blew on his tea to cool it. "We have a lot to talk about," he said.

"Yes, we do." Best to agree. "But we have lots of time, don't we?" *But Jim doesn't. Play your cards right, Andrea.* "We don't need to have hard feelings about the past, do we?"

Robert's eyebrows rose. "No, we certainly don't. I knew you really wanted to be with me, but *he* had some kind of hold on you."

"Well, I think you could be right. I think I could let it all go now. Could you?" *Oh no. I'm moving too fast. He'll know I don't mean it.* "I mean, it will take some time to get used to the change, and we have things to work out, but I'm willing to try. Are you?"

"Of course. You're my wife. We belong together." His nostrils flared slightly.

"Yes, yes, of course." I reached out and tentatively patted his hand, willing mine not to tremble. "Only it's going to take time to talk things through and get back on track. You understand that, don't you?" I gave him another pat, all the while terrified that he might grab my hand and twist my wrist. I played mind games with myself to push away my fear.

"That's right." He lifted my hand, kissed my fingers, and set it back down. I let my relieved breath out ever so slowly.

"There's one thing though that's going to bother me, Robert."

He frowned. "What's that?"

"Years from now, I'm always going to have a bad feeling about what you've done to Jim, letting him die out there." There! I said it. *Please, please don't get mad.*

Robert's eyes narrowed to slits and I braced myself for a backhand wallop, but I was determined not to cringe visibly. Inside, I was totally cringing, but I kept a straight face.

"Thought you didn't care about him anymore. We're together again." His voice was louder as he set his mug down harder than necessary.

"No, I don't, but it just isn't right for one human being to do that to another, and you're not like that. I know you're not that mean." *Not much. Oh God, what a liar I can be.*

"Hmpf! I'll think about it."

"He doesn't have much time."

Robert's fist slammed the table. "I said I'll think about it. Now drop it!"

When the fist came down, my resolve to be tough flew out the window. I couldn't help jumping from fright. *Quickly! Pull yourself together, or you're lost.*

I looked at the table so Robert would not be able to read any emotion on my face. "All right, Robert. It's okay. We don't have to think about it right now." *How can I think of anything else?* "Do you have any cookies on the boat?" *Distract him.*

"Cookies? Uh … er … no. But I have some crackers and peanut butter." He started to get up.

"No, no, no, it's okay. I'll get them. Just tell me where they are." *Kowtow. It's what he likes.* I got the crackers and put some peanut butter on one and offered it to him.

He looked pleased and surprised. "Thank you."

I spread peanut butter on one for myself. "Are you planning on leaving in the morning?"

"Yup. First light. We can make it to Rupert tomorrow."

"Okay, will we be going to get groceries there and fuel?" I remembered the routine from last year and hoped it sounded as if I was looking forward to the trip.

"Just like last year," he said, smiling.

"Yes, just like last year. Except you'll have a murder hanging over your head. You don't want that, do you?"

Robert turned his head to the side and grimaced. "I'm having a hard time believing you, Andrea. You keep wanting to save that sonofabitch." His cheek muscles were working hard.

"You don't understand, Robert. Please, believe me. I just don't want to think that you'd do something like that. Leaving a person for dead. You could just go up there and get his skiff back to him and then he can be on his own. Sink or swim, right? It wouldn't be your fault then, whatever happens." I held my breath.

"I'll think about it. But right now I have a headache. You'll have to go down into the lower bunk for a while and I'm going to lie down."

"Okay, but you don't have to lock the door, do you? I mean if we're really going to be together again?"

He hesitated, and then relented. "All right. I guess that way we'll find out if you're being honest with me. Go ahead. Go downstairs and I won't lock the door, but I've got to lie down. Just for an hour. This migraine is coming on like a freight train."

I hurried down the three steps to the fo'c'sle and climbed onto the bed there. I listened as Robert lay down on the bunk and let out a long sigh and a groan. I turned my face to the wall and thought about the last time I lay in this bunk. I was locked in after a failed attempt to run away with Jim, doubled up in pain from the beating Robert dished out, and burned on the hand when I tried to catch myself from falling into the stovetop. My loving husband and I were back together unless some miracle happened and Jim survived. In the darkness I let my tears flow. *Oh, my poor Jim. I tried, I tried.*

Chapter 53

I was fuming with futile anger. I was useless. I was stupid to let my guard down about Robert. I was stupid long before that, not to realize the tide would run into the flats so quickly. I knew better. What the hell was wrong with me? And how stupid was I to let Robert take Andrea. Robert was always strange, but he was getting really psychotic. He wasn't just your regular wife beater. He had a few screws loose and more loosening all the time. Andrea was in real danger. I had to save her.

The water trickled over the tops of my boots and I was standing on the higher ground, not in a ditch. If I was going to save Andrea, I would first have to save myself.

Robert was sure he had left me for dead. If I didn't do some fast thinking, he would be right. I had my survival pack with me but foolishly I had left the handheld VHF on the boat. There wasn't much chance it would do any good anyway. Hemmed in by mountains, I had no one near to call except Robert. It wasn't an option. But I had my bear spray and my inflatable lifejacket. Not that the lifejacket would do much good in these icy waters. A body was only good for a few minutes before hypothermia set in. Didn't matter if you could swim or not. And that river came straight off the glaciers of the interior. Ice cold even in May. It wasn't very wide though, and maybe not too deep all the way across.

As the tide came in I backed up more and more towards the treeline. Those standing trees probably weren't underwater very often, so that might be a good place to head for until the tide started to go out again. It would be dusk soon and I should find a place. Or … I could take the bull by the horns and go the other way, towards where my skiff was jammed up on the opposite side of the river. Might be better to do that before hypothermia set in.

I waded across the ditches that had filled and walked through a foot of water that had flooded the higher grassy area. My boots had filled with water long ago, but at least the initial deep cold was gone, having sucked up some of my body heat at the same time. Soon I saw the skiff wedged in among some small trees that had fallen down the gravelly bank on the other side of the river. I found a place where the river was narrowest and decided to go for it. I inflated my life vest, cinched up my backpack tightly—I might need it yet—and waded into the river. I was disappointed that it got deep fairly quickly. Once I got thigh deep and it was still dropping off, I launched myself into the flow and swam like hell. I couldn't afford to stay in that water for long. Fuck it was cold.

My waterlogged boots were dragging me down, making my kicking ineffectual, but at least the life vest held me up. My arms did a lot of the work of getting me across the river. They were soon aching with the exertion and cold. In a way, the flow of the river helped me get across, as long as I didn't worry about trying to go in a straight line. On the other side, I stretched my legs down for a foothold and thanked my lucky stars that I found it. That made scrambling out the other side faster than trying to swim a few more frigid strokes.

The current had swept me downstream just enough that I was close to the skiff. It was wedged right into the tangle of trees with the motor completely submerged but the front of the skiff was out of the water. My teeth were chattering and my arms shook as I pulled on the bow and set the boat more securely on the bank. The Ziploc bag under the seat had kept the handheld VHF dry. I retrieved that and set it aside. Now on the riverbank, I was able to tip the skiff sideways to drain most of the water. The oars were still in the oarlocks. I'm sure Robert didn't expect me to get to the skiff to have the option of using the oars, or he would have thrown them out.

It was nearly dark by the time I got the skiff into the water. My whole body was vibrating as I pulled on the oars and rowed myself back to the Serenity. I could barely manage to tie the painter to the davits. With every muscle shivering, climbing aboard the boat was a challenge. *Just one more effort and then you'll be in the warm boat. Come on, Jim. Find some strength. You still have to save Andrea.* I heaved myself up onto the deck and collapsed there. *Get up! Get up or you'll still die after all this!* I crawled into the wheelhouse. Luckily I had the usual kettle of water on the top of the stove. I didn't even look for a tea bag—just poured myself a cup of hot water, spilling half of it with my shaking hands, and drank it down. Then I stripped off my wet clothes, got into my Stanfield underwear—wool for warmth—poured another cup of hot water and crawled into my bunk to warm up.

There was no question of going to sleep. I was only in the bunk to get warm and get my strength back. After about an hour, I got dressed in warm dry clothes and put on a pair of runners. I took my bear spray and handheld VHF, just in case, and climbed back into the skiff.

Robert had said he was just around the corner from us and I was pretty sure he wouldn't be going anywhere until the next day. The bastard would want to enjoy Andrea first, and he wouldn't want to risk having to keep her under control while he was running the boat at night. Anyway, he wouldn't be worrying that I was a threat anymore. He'd be pretty sure I'd be dead soon.

I rowed quietly and kept close to shore. Sound carries on the water and since we were alone in the inlet, any noise Robert might hear would make him suspicious. A few hours ago, darkness could have posed a big problem for me, but now it worked in my favour. So did the tide. It had turned and I was rowing with the outgoing tide. My only problem would be to get to the stern of the Hawkeye without him seeing me. His boat would have swung away from the anchor and his bow would be facing into the inlet so he could see me if he happened to look.

I hugged the shoreline, blending into the darkness of the trees behind me, until I was near enough to row across towards the Hawkeye. I worked the oars cautiously and quietly. When I was near his stern I worked one oar to put me closer and then made a grab for one of the davits at the stern of his boat. I tied the painter onto it and then sat a moment to listen.

I could hear every word. After all, I was only a few feet away, huddled in the skiff in the dark behind the stern. It wasn't the safest place for me to stay for long. I would be at a severe disadvantage if Robert noticed me there.

"Is your headache gone?" I heard Andrea ask.

"Just about," he answered. "Almost gone. Too much stress, I guess."

Andrea's voice was soothing. "Can I get you anything?"

"Not right now. I'll let you know," he said, "but first I want to know why you ran off?"

"I felt bad about that," Andrea said, "but I was afraid."

Robert's voice was alternately pleading and bullying. To her credit, Andrea kept her tone level. She'd had a lot of practice in what to do and not to do around Robert. While they talked, I climbed up on the stern of the boat, being careful to board in the center so the Hawkeye wouldn't rock with my weight and tip Robert off. I looked around for a weapon. I had the bear spray with me, but I wanted to have something extra in case the spray was knocked out of my hand. Two gaffs hung on the inside of the cockpit just by my feet. I picked up one of them, careful not to make a sound. I didn't think I could bring myself to use the sharp hook of the gaff on Robert, no matter how much I hated him, but I didn't mind whacking him on the head with the club part of it, like stunning a fish before gaffing it.

I could feel my pulse throbbing at the side of my temple, keeping time with my pounding chest. I couldn't screw this up. I tiptoed over to the darker side of the boat away from the light flooding out from the open wheelhouse door. In the darkness I worried I might trip over something and give myself away. I stood in the blackness of the night and wondered what my next step should be. I knew I would have a better chance of tackling Robert outside on the deck. Inside the wheelhouse too much could go wrong.

Eventually he would come out on deck to take a piss, but that could be a while. I decided to make a noise and have him come out to investigate. Better to have the noise come from the side away from me. I looked around for something to throw, but Robert was so tidy, there was nothing lying around. I reached over towards the wheelhouse door and used the length of the gaff to bang the wall under the doorsill, and then I slipped back into the darkness and waited, my heart pounding in my throat.

A chair lurched and must have fallen over in the galley. Robert came charging out onto the deck and stood looking around. He saw my skiff tied to the stern and spun around to look for me. I gave him a blast with the bear spray, but he threw himself at me as if it had no effect on him. I swung the gaff. It glanced off his shoulder and went clattering onto the deck. I had forgotten how big he was. His fist crashed into my head, knocking my glasses off. I lay across the hatch cover, stunned, and looked up at Robert's face.

"You sonofabitch," he yelled. "Looks like I'll have to finish you off with my bare hands."

I rolled sideways and sat up, still dazed. "Bring it on then."

His eyes were wide with fury, but they squinted shut when a spasm of coughing overtook him. The pepper spray hung in the air and we both had coughing fits. Robert's rage rose above the effects of the pepper spray and again he raised his fist. In a split second it would crash into my face and that would be the end of my rescue attempt.

Andrea shrieked hysterically, "No! Robert! Don't! Stop!" She had picked up the gaff and flailed it at him. Then she bent over, coughing violently, dropping the gaff as she gasped for air. I scrambled up just as Robert made a lunge for Andrea. She took a quick step to the side, and Robert changed direction to go for her. He stepped on the gaff which rolled and threw him off balance. His big body hurtled towards the cap railing. He grabbed for the trolling pole before going overboard, hitting his head on the metal bracket that supported the pole.

"Robert!" Andrea shouted. "Jim! Throw him a life ring."

I jumped up onto the wheelhouse roof to fetch the life ring and tossed it out into the darkness. I listened for the sound of water splashing, but heard nothing. "Robert?" I called. "Robert? Can you hear me?" Silence.

I went into the wheelhouse and turned on the spotlight, turning it in all directions. Andrea found a flashlight in the tools drawer. She went out on deck to shine it around closer to the sides of the boat where the spotlight couldn't reach.

We strained our ears, listening for splashing or heavy breathing. Nothing. Only the sound of the water swishing and lapping at the skiffs tied to the Hawkeye, Robert's at the side and mine at the stern.

I shone the spotlight around again, farther out this time, looking for a body, but he must have sunk quickly after knocking himself out.

"No use," I said, after searching all around the boat. "Look at this." I pointed at the base of the trolling pole. "He really smashed his head. Blood on the stanchion."

"He must have sunk right away," Andrea said. "Do you think he's under the boat?

"The way this tide is running out, he'll have been swept right along with it, out of this bay into Grenville Channel. There, the bottom drops away steeply. It would be like falling off an underwater cliff. He'll sink so deep, they'll never find him."

"When he refused to go back and bring you a skiff, I prayed for a reckoning. Now the same tide that he thought would kill you has turned and swept him out of our lives forever."

~

Oh, there will be a reckoning,
As sure as you were born.
The power and control you sought
Have rendered you forlorn.

I may have loved you at one time,
It faded all too fast.
Your cruelty degraded me,
I wished for times long past.

The tide has turned, your fate is sealed,
Your wicked plan has failed.
At last there is a reckoning,
And justice has prevailed.

~

www.ingramcontent.com/pod-product-compliance
Lightning Source LLC
Chambersburg PA
CBHW032005050726
47590CB00006B/2055